HIS OBSESSION

THE HUNTER BROTHERS BOOK 1

M. S. PARKER

BELMONTE PUBLISHING, LLC

This book is a work of fiction. The names, characters, places and incidents are products of the writer's imagination or have been used fictitiously and are not to be construed as real. Any resemblance to persons, living or dead, actual events, locales or organizations is entirely coincidental.

Copyright © 2018 Belmonte Publishing LLC

Published by Belmonte Publishing LLC

READING ORDER

Thank you so much for reading His Obsession, the first book in the Hunter Brothers series. All books in the series can be read stand-alone, but if you'd like to read the complete series, I recommend reading them in this order:

1. His Obsession
2. His Control (March 28)
3. His Hunger (April 25)
4. His Secret (May 23)

PROLOGUE

Manfred

Nothing could compare to a glass of Highland Park scotch after a long day at work. In fact, the only thing that could've made it better would have been if Olive hadn't been visiting her sister in Greece. I knew she missed Diana, but dammit, I missed my wife.

I clipped the end of my cigar and stuck it in my mouth. At least I didn't have to hear her lecturing me about smoking in the house, I thought as I lit it. I rarely indulged, but now seemed like as good a time as any. I'd closed my deal with McOmber Shipping at half the original asking price. If my crew did as good a job with this company as they had with the last, they'd be getting an even bigger beginning-of-the-year bonus than usual.

I was just getting settled in front of the fireplace, ready to crack open the latest Grisham novel, when the doorbell sounded. I hated the damn thing, but the house was too big to hear anyone knock unless we were right there. Olive insisted the chimes made her smile, but I didn't want to smile when I opened my front door. I wanted to know who the hell was showing up without calling first. Not that I would've ever told Olive that. I'd do whatever was necessary to keep her happy, so if the damn chimes made her happy, then I wouldn't complain about them.

The doorbell went off again, and I pushed myself out of my chair. If it was some Girl Scout selling cookies, then I'd buy a box of thin mints and send her on her way, but anyone else was going to get an earful.

Except when I opened the door, it wasn't a person standing on the other side. It was two people. Two police officers. Uniformed ones. With matching grim expressions on their faces. But these weren't the sort of grim expressions that came with men who'd been sent to ask for money for a policemen's fund. These made my entire body go cold.

"Mr. Hunter," one of them spoke, shifting from one foot to the other like whatever it was he had to say made it impossible for him to stand still. "Mr. Hunter, there's been an accident."

"Olive?" I could barely breathe. "My wife? Is she...?"

"Not your wife, Mr. Hunter." The other officer took over. He met my eyes for a moment before looking away. "I'm afraid it's your son."

Chester.

Blood rushed in my ears.

"Your son, your daughter-in-law, and their children were in a car accident tonight. We're here to take you to the hospital." I took a step forward, but the cop who had been speaking held up his hand. "Sir, you'll want a coat. It's cold out."

I nodded and turned back inside. I barely registered anything I was doing. All I could think about was my boy and his family. It had to be bad for cops to come here to get me, but if they were all dead, it wouldn't have been two uniforms. I was friends with the commissioner and the mayor. I knew the governor. If my family was dead, surely one of them would've come instead.

"When did...how long..." I couldn't quite form a full question even though I had a thousand of them running through my head.

"We were sent out almost immediately after the first responders arrived at the scene." The officer who'd been doing most of the talking opened the back door of their car, so I could get in. "One of them recognized your son's name and called into the station. We were the closest to your place."

"Does that mean you don't know much about what happened?" I wasn't sure if I was hoping that they didn't know any details, so I could imagine things weren't actually bad enough for me to need a police escort to the hospital, or if it'd be better to know so I couldn't imagine worse things.

"It was bad," the first man said. "That's all we know right now. They'll know more at the hospital."

Something about the way he said it told me he was lying, and I decided that knowing wasn't as bad as imagining. "Tell me."

A moment of silence passed as the two men looked at each other, and my insides knotted.

"Your daughter-in-law and granddaughter were DOA."

While I appreciated him not sugarcoating things, it didn't make the blow hurt any less. Abigail, gone. She and Chester had been in love from the moment they first met. And now she was gone. And Aimee.

I couldn't bear it. My only granddaughter. Four years old.

All that life, all that potential. Gone.

My chest was so tight I could barely breathe.

"Your son is on his way to the hospital," the officer continued. "And so's your grandson, but I don't know details about them."

Relief rushed through me, followed by guilt, and then both

nearly choked me. I was struggling to process it when what he said registered.

"Grandson?" I leaned forward, clenching my hands. "What about the other boys?"

"What other boys, Mr. Hunter?" the quieter cop asked.

"I have four grandsons." Even as I said the words, I prayed they were still true.

"There were only two kids in the car," the other guy picked it up again.

"Where are the other kids?" My lips felt numb. Everything felt numb.

"We'll find them," he promised. "I'll radio it in right now."

I nodded. Chester would need to know that his kids...his *boys* were safe. When I got to the hospital, that's what I would tell him first. That the boys were safe. I wouldn't tell him about his daughter until I knew he'd make it.

He had to make it.

I closed my eyes. How was I going to tell Olive that Abigail and Aimee were dead? I couldn't even think about it.

"What happened?" The question slipped out before I could stop it.

"Black ice."

If I still had my eyes closed, I wouldn't have seen the way the officer in the passenger's seat looked over at the driver. Like there was something about that answer he wasn't comfortable with. Right now, I would've jumped at anything that meant I didn't have to think about the overseas call I needed to make tonight.

"You don't agree?"

He looked back at me, then to his partner, then back to me. "I don't know, Mr. Hunter. It's possible that the car hit a patch of ice." He paused before adding, "But something about it doesn't sit right with me. I think there's something else going on."

Something else? What did he mean by that?

I didn't get a chance to ask since we were pulling into the hospital's parking lot, but somehow, I knew this conversation would come back to me many times in the weeks and months that followed.

ONE
JAX

Twenty-Four Years Later...

Mid-January in New York City was fucking cold. I was from Boston, so it wasn't like I wasn't used to real winters, but there was something about New York City that always made me feel twice as cold.

"Damn!" The man following me out of the building apparently agreed with me.

I glanced over my shoulder to see Justin McManus blowing on his hands like he'd been walking outside for a while rather than having just left the comfortably warm offices that Hunter Enterprises held here in the Big Apple. That wasn't surprising since McManus was a Jacksonville native, and living up north for a decade hadn't made a difference.

"I'm going for a drink," he said as he stepped up to the curb and held up a hand to hail a cab. "Would you like to join me?"

I had a plane to catch in the morning, but my flight wasn't insanely early, and I didn't have a reason to head back to my hotel room right away. Normally, I wouldn't have even gotten a room since the company plane was generally available whenever I needed it. Unfortunately, there'd been some sort of mechanical issue with the plane, which meant I was subject to the whims of airport scheduling for this trip.

I agreed amiably and followed Justin into a taxi, letting him fill the silence as he usually did. We weren't close, and I wasn't even sure I could classify him as a friend, but of all the board members, he was the closest one to my age – thirty-seven to my thirty-two – and the only other non-native New Yorker, which pretty much made the two of us outsiders. And we didn't even attempt to discuss sports.

I was a Celtics and Red Sox fan, so I knew better than to even ask where others' loyalties lay.

"How's your grandfather?"

Justin's question caught my attention, drawing my attention back to him. "He's good," I said. "I'll let him know you asked about him."

Justin gave me one of his typical charming smiles. "I've only met him once. I doubt he'll remember me, but he sure made an impression on me."

"He remembers you," I assured him. "He knows the name of every executive at Hunter Enterprises and most of the other employees too. I may handle most of the day-to-day business anymore, but he's still as sharp as ever."

"I'll bet it was hell getting him to retire."

I laughed and shook my head. "I'll *catch* hell if I ever use that word in his presence. Eighty-one years old, and if he runs out of paperwork to look over, he comes into the office and starts re-arranging the lobby."

"Your brothers aren't helping?"

The smile dropped from my face, and he must've realized that he stepped in something because he immediately started back-peddling.

"I mean, I heard that you had three brothers, but I've never seen them at any of the business functions."

"It's all right." I managed to give him a tight smile. It wasn't his fault that my brothers had all cut and run as soon as they were able. "They aren't involved in the family business."

I could see Justin trying to figure out the best way to respond, mentally debating if he should change the subject or acknowledge what I said. Fortunately, we pulled up to the bar just then, and it was easy to wait until we were inside to turn the conversation to alcohol.

Fortunately, alcohol was exactly what I needed right now.

WHILE I WASN'T unaccustomed to a drink of good scotch after a hard day of work, I rarely drank enough to have anything more than a relaxing effect. Tonight, I'd indulged a bit more than usual, and I felt better than relaxed. I was...buzzed.

Even though it was closing in on ten o'clock, and logic told me that the temperature had dropped, the air felt almost warm as I stepped outside. Well, not *warm*, but invigorating rather than bracing. So much so that I decided to take a walk before heading to my hotel. There wasn't anything to do there but sleep anyway.

I gave Justin a farewell nod and then started down the sidewalk without any real idea of where I was going. I had a private gym back home, so I was in great shape, but I didn't really do much regular walking. In Boston, I had a car service I regularly used, and a car of my own for the rare occasions I felt like driving. Sometimes, when I was at work and wanted to go out for lunch, I'd walk, but I never did it for the sheer enjoyment of walking.

It seemed like I never did much of anything for sheer enjoyment anymore.

I frowned, not liking the maudlin directions my thoughts were taking me, but unable to stop them. Justin had planted the seed with his innocuous questions about my grandfather and my brothers, and now that I was out of the noise of the bar, I couldn't quite keep the thoughts back.

I'd moved into the dorms when I was at Harvard, then gotten a small apartment of my own, but when I started thinking about upgrading, I decided to give in to the inevitable and had officially bought the family home from Grandfather a few years ago when it became clear that he'd never agree to downsize. He had an entire floor to himself, and it was almost like living on my own.

Except I wasn't on my own. I was back under my grandfather's roof, and by my own choice this time. Sometimes, I could still feel it, that sense of anger and grief so sharp that it was like my eight-year-old self had never truly left me. I hadn't shown it back then, and I didn't show it now, but on nights when I couldn't sleep, I'd feel that little kid inside me wanting to scream and rage at the unfairness of it all.

The worst part had been the people who acted like, because my brothers and I had a rich grandfather to take us in, the pain of losing both of our parents and our sister had somehow been less.

I shoved my hands into my coat pockets and hunched against a sudden gust of wind.

Even though Grandfather and I lived in the same house, I rarely saw him. The times he came into the office didn't even change that much. We communicated largely via email, with the occasional phone call, and that wasn't much different than how he did things while I was growing up.

I definitely got my work ethic from him.

And I wasn't the only one.

As many issues as I had with my brothers, they all worked hard. Cai was a doctor slash scientist working for the Center for Disease Control in Atlanta. Slade lived in El Paso and worked as a DEA agent. Even Blake, who'd taken a less traditional route, made a good enough living selling his handcrafted products that he didn't even need to touch his dividends from his share in the company.

At least that's what I assumed they were all still doing. I hadn't seen them in more than three years, and our contact since then had come in brief texts and emails. Even on Christmas, I'd sent each of them the same short message, and received back the sort of reply my texts deserved.

"Great way to kill a buzz," I muttered to myself. It was time to get a taxi and go back to the hotel. If I stayed out here any longer, I was going to start thinking about why my brothers and I barely spoke anymore, and that was never a good path to take.

I started to raise my hand to flag down a cab when I saw her.

Long golden curls peeking out from under a hat. Average height and build, but something about the set of her jaw and the way she carried herself got my attention. I hadn't come to New York with the intention of getting laid, but sex would definitely get my mind off things.

I dropped my hand and started after the blonde.

TWO
SYLL

"If you don't put that cigarette out this instant, I'm going to make you eat it."

As the asshole with the Marlboro light gave me a slow once-over, I could read on his face what he was thinking. Barely over five feet, with curves but no discernable muscle, I wasn't exactly the most intimidating person in the room, but he was new here, so I could excuse him for underestimating me.

What I couldn't excuse was him smoking in my bar.

"Why don't you head over to the bar and bring me a drink?" He winked at me – actually fucking *winked* at me – and then added, "And I wouldn't say no to your number."

"Listen here, you little fucker!"

Gilly Snowe shouldn't have been any more intimidating than me, but something about her tended to scare the shit out of people. The smoker was no exception.

His eyes went wide, and he immediately stubbed out his cigarette and threw up his hands in front of him. "It's out! Chill!"

I could've told him that was one of the absolute worst things he could have said to Gilly, but then I wouldn't have had the pleasure of watching her grab the guy's ear, yank him up out of his seat, and drag him over to the door.

"You want to smoke, you go outside to do it," she said. "And you treat that woman with respect. After all, she owns the bar."

The guy looked at me, and I shrugged. It wasn't my fault he assumed I was a waitress. I may have owned the place, but I wasn't too proud to work in it. Hell, I'd been working here for as long as I could remember. Definitely before it'd technically been legal, but since Dad had owned the place, and he'd kept me away from the alcohol, nobody'd said much of anything about it.

"Now that we've come to an understanding," Gilly released the man's ear, "I think you should buy everyone a round as an apology for stinking up the place."

When Gilly got like this, it always made me wonder what sort of life she'd come from. For as long as I could remember, she'd been here, but I knew she wasn't a native to Boston. I'd heard the story once or twice over the years, how she'd come to the bar for work and hadn't left until my dad had given her a job. She was almost like the big sister I never had, and with Dad gone, she was pretty much my only family.

The pain in my chest was familiar after two years. It hadn't gone away, just faded into the background where I could forget about it for a while.

No, not forget. I could never forget about my father. It'd been almost two years since he died, and whenever I thought about him, it felt like yesterday.

I looked around my bar – *his* bar – and smiled at each of the customers even though I knew it didn't make it to my eyes. I looked like him. The same olive-green color, and the same cocoa-brown waves of hair too. I didn't remember my mother, and I didn't see any of her in my reflection either. But Dad? Him, I saw everywhere.

"Miss Reeve?" I turned to see the smoker standing in front of me, his cheeks red, eyes downcast. "I'm sorry."

I nodded once, then headed back behind the bar. I didn't usually come out onto the floor unless absolutely necessary, but when I saw that idiot lighting up in here, I hadn't thought twice. Even back before all the smoking laws, my dad had banned smoking in the bar because he hadn't wanted me breathing in all that crap.

"Fucking tourists," Gilly said as she came by to pick up a tray of drinks. "Come in here, acting like they own the fucking place." Her green eyes snapped angrily.

I reached across the bar and put my hand on her arm. "You know as well as I do that those tourists are keeping us afloat."

"We have our regulars." She pushed back the curls from her face and leaned on the bar.

"We do," I agreed. "But they aren't drinking as much as they used to, and the ones that are, aren't drinking the same quality they used to."

She opened her mouth like she was going to argue, because that was what Gilly did. She argued with me. But not right now because there wasn't anything she could say. Because she knew it was true. I loved our regulars, loved the way they remembered my dad, but they weren't making ends meet anymore.

"I need a Dark & Stormy, a French Connection, and a Park Avenue." Ariene Sward threw the drink orders at me with a toss of her bottle-blonde hair. "And you might want to hurry it up."

I would've been hurrying to do just that if she hadn't told me to do it like she was my boss instead of the other way around. Ariene had only been a waitress here for a few months, but she liked to pretend that she could do whatever she wanted. At least once a week I had to do something to remind her that she wasn't nearly as important as she thought she was. It sounded harsh, I knew, but she skated the line of what was acceptable behavior for an employee.

I purposefully pulled up two bottles of beer and reached around Ariene to hand them to Gilly. "Angus and Tommy look like they're getting low over there."

"Yes, ma'am." Gilly's words had an undercurrent of amusement, but she didn't say anything else as she took the bottles.

I ignored the glare Ariene sent my way as I set about making the drinks she requested. I would've loved to fire her and find someone else, but I didn't have the time or the energy to train another new waitress. That was another reason the bar's finances were stretched thin. I couldn't compete with other places willing and able to pay more.

"Here." I put the last glass on the tray. "And when you're done, pick up the extra glasses and take them back to the kitchen. If you need them, wash them up."

Ariene puffed out an annoyed breath. "I thought you hired me as a waitress, not as a dishwasher. I didn't apply to wash dishes."

I raised an eyebrow and looked up at her. "If you read your terms of employment, you'd know that you were hired primarily as a waitress, but to also do other things as needed. The first one on that list was dishwashing."

Her cheeks flushed, but she didn't say anything. She wasn't stupid, just spoiled. She knew she'd pushed me as far as she could today. Especially since Gilly was glaring at her from across the room. The two couldn't stand each other, and I knew it wouldn't take much provocation for Gilly to throw Ariene out on her ass.

And now, I wouldn't be too disinclined to stop her.

"You look exhausted," Gilly announced as she came behind the bar to pour her own drinks. "You need to get some sleep."

I didn't bother to respond. She was only six years older than my own twenty-four, but she'd been mothering me since the moment we first met. Making sure I ate, slept, took care of myself. Or she tried to as best she could anyway. I didn't always listen.

"Hey, babe, got a cold one for me?"

If I hadn't recognized his voice, I would've known he'd come in by the chill I could feel coming from Gilly.

Billy Outhwaite and I had been dating since I was a senior in high school. Seven years. Most people thought we'd be married by now, but I was glad he never popped the question. I would've had to say no. I loved him, sure, but I wasn't sure I could live with him. We both liked our space.

"How did things go today?" I asked as he came up behind me and wrapped his arm around my waist. He kissed the top of my head and ground his crotch against my ass while I tried not to roll my eyes. We'd talked about his PDA before, but he always came back to *babe, I can't help it if you get me hot and bothered*, and any arguments about appropriate public behavior got lost in him turning the whole conversation into how I just didn't understand how much he needed to show me he loved me.

"Not bad," he said as he kissed the side of my neck. "Benji said he'd put in a good word for me with his boss."

I clenched my jaw and stepped to the side, moving out of his embrace. Billy had been unemployed for nearly eight months now, and every time I asked him how the job search was going, it was like this. He'd say something non-committal, and then talk about some friend of his who was going to 'put in a good word with his boss.'

I reminded myself that all relationships had their ups and downs, then I smiled and got back to work.

THREE
JAX

I was starting to feel like I'd crossed into stalking territory when the blonde suddenly turned toward what looked like a club. It didn't have a long line in front of it, but it did have a massive man standing in front of the door. Like arms the size of bowling balls massive.

And he just stepped aside and let the blonde in without a word.

I scowled, but still had enough of a buzz to try to follow inside. The still-rational part of my brain, while small, reasoned that I'd be turned away, at which point I'd take a cab and go back to my hotel. If I was still feeling like getting laid, I'd check out the hotel bar.

But the guy didn't tell me to get lost. Instead, he looked me over, handed me a paper, and then opened the door for me. Surprised, I didn't bother looking at the paper as I walked inside to what looked like a lobby, with a second door on the far side.

This guy wasn't as big as the first one, but he wasn't small either. Unlike the other one, he didn't move from in front of the door when I approached.

"Read it. Sign it."

I waited for further instructions, but he didn't say anything else.

So, I looked down at the paper in my hand. "Welcome to guest night at Club Privé."

Club Privé?

I'd never heard of it. But it *was* something new, and I didn't get a lot of new in my life. The rest of the flyer was some standard legal jargon about how everything at the club was required to be safe and consensual, and that the club reserved the right to ask anyone not following the rules to leave.

I signed it, handed it over, and then walked inside.

If I hadn't been slightly drunk, the words *safe and consensual* might have clued me into what was in store. As it was, though, I didn't realize that Club Privé was a sex club until I was already inside.

And not just any sex club, but a BDSM sex club.

All around me, men and women walked by, some of them dressed in the skimpy clothes you'd normally see at any club... but others were in leather and chains...or not much else at all.

I couldn't believe I'd just stumbled into a BDSM club that looked like the sort of place I'd been dreaming of since I'd first learned just how much this kind of thing turned me on. There were a couple places in Boston that catered to my particular preferences, but nothing like this.

I took a few steps away from the door and turned slowly, taking in everything around me. It was a massive space, with high ceilings and randomly placed pillars. Instead of pulsing strobe lights, the entire space was lit with what looked to be blue and white Christmas lights. The colors were softer than anything I'd seen in a club before. The music was like that too. Instead of harsh dance music, this was low enough that people could talk over the pulsing beat. Long, low couches were scattered around, as were regular tables and chairs. In the center of the room was a dance floor where several couples were already swaying slowly.

"Damn," I whistled softly. Back home, if I wanted to hook up with someone who was into BDSM, I'd go to a club, but that's all it ever was. I never really liked spending time there. This place, I'd come to just to relax.

If I hadn't been looking for sex. And I was, now more than ever.

I turned my attention from the club and started looking for the hot blonde again. Maybe once she and I hooked up, I'd take a closer look at the club, figure out who owned it, and how to contact them.

Club Privé sounded like it'd be a good business to buy in New York.

After a moment, I spotted her. The blonde was standing next to the bar, talking with the bartender, but no man had approached her yet. Perfect. I walked straight toward her, appreciating the view with each step. I stepped just inside her personal space and leaned on the bar.

"What drink am I buying you?"

She looked over at me, surprised, either by the way I phrased it, or by the offer itself, though I couldn't imagine I was the first man who'd ever bought her a drink. She had brown eyes, I saw, like melted chocolate.

"I'm not interested," she said politely. "But thank you."

I grinned. A challenge. I liked that. "One drink. Come on."

She gave me a sideways look, then held up her left hand. For a moment, I thought she was flipping me off, but then I saw what was on her finger. A pair of platinum rings, one with a very large diamond in it.

Oh.

"I didn't know," I said, straightening.

She lifted a brow. "I hope that's true."

A man's voice came from behind me, and I turned to see a tall, muscular man with dark hair and a scowl. The fact that he looked like he wanted to kill me made me think he was probably the blonde's husband.

Shit.

"I didn't," I said, taking a step back.

One of the reasons I rarely got drunk was because, the first time I'd done it, I'd learned that the filter from my brain to my mouth didn't work as well as it should when I consumed too much alcohol.

Which meant it was no surprise when I opened my mouth and something stupid came out. "Just a piece of advice. If you have a wife that fine, putting a ring on it doesn't do shit if you're not around to be man enough to keep it."

The man took a step toward me, but the blonde put her hand on his chest. "Gavin, he's drunk and running his mouth. Let it go."

"Right," I said. "Let it go. I have business to attend to anyway."

"Business?" The scowl hadn't faded much yet. "Here?"

I nodded. "I intend to make an offer to the owner of this club."

Gavin crossed his arms and gave me a look that said if his wife hadn't been standing next to him, he would've broken my jaw. "Offer?"

"I want to buy this place."

I made the pronouncement and then waited for someone to say something, maybe give me the guy's name at least.

Instead, Gavin grabbed the back of my coat and started pulling me to the door. The first bouncer looked startled when we walked by but followed us. The second guy simply said, "Boss?"

I had a bad feeling I was in deep shit.

"*My* club isn't for sale, asshole."

Yep, deep shit, I thought as Gavin shoved me onto the sidewalk.

Could've been worse, I supposed. I could've found out she was married *after* I fucked her.

FOUR
SYLL

I slapped at my alarm clock, missed, and then reminded myself that I'd moved it from my bedside table to avoid this exact scenario. Groaning, I sat up and blearily made my way across my tiny bedroom to the trunk I used as a dresser. I smacked the top of my clock, and the obnoxious fire-alarm blaring finally stopped. I'd never been a morning person and keeping bar hours hadn't helped. In school, my phone had been enough to get me up, but not anymore. If things kept going this way, I'd need one of those alarm clocks that ran when they went off, so I'd have to chase it.

Just the thought made me want to climb back under the covers.

Instead, I trudged into the bathroom and began my morning routine.

It was nearly noon, but since I was just waking up, it was breakfast time for me. Not that I was particularly picky about what I was eating. Dry cereal, oatmeal, a ham and cheese sandwich...I didn't care as long as I had a cup of coffee.

I was lucky I could remember my name if I wasn't caffeinated.

I carried my raisin-covered oatmeal and giant mug of coffee from my kitchenette into my office. When my dad moved us into the space behind the bar after my mom left, he converted a space between the back of the bar and the front into an office. It had allowed him to keep most of his work life separate from our personal life, and I still used it the same way. Granted, I didn't really have much of a personal life, but it did help me keep a definite start and finish to my days, long as they were.

I went through the easy stuff while my brain absorbed the caffeine. Checked emails. Bank account. That sort of thing. I marked everything I needed to come back to or take a closer look at, and then I pulled out the books. My dad had done things old school, and that was how he taught me to do them too, but when I took over the accounting a few years back, I made a deal with him. I'd keep the old books, but I'd use new ones as well. It allowed me to double-check everything, and it made me feel a bit more secure about doing it all on my own. Someone might get access to one set of my books, but I doubted anyone could get both.

It took about an hour before the numbers started to blur, not because it'd taken me that long to see if things added up, but because I'd been trying to find places where I could save money, and I'd come up with squat.

Less than squat.

Shit.

When my dad was alive, we served food from five to seven every night. Nothing fancy, but some of the best hamburgers in the area, and the fries hadn't been too bad either. Dad had manned the grill himself, and I made random desserts whenever I didn't have too much homework. Cookies and cakes, with an occasional pie thrown in. I was no Betty Crocker, but the regulars had loved it.

But after Dad died – a heart-attack at only fifty-two – I hadn't had the heart to even consider replacing him. By the time

I'd grieved enough to be able to walk into the bar without bursting into tears, things had changed. Some of the people I counted on being there for me had disappeared, finding another bar to haunt, maybe somewhere they didn't have to worry about it closing for a week while a daughter mourned.

It had been a couple of months before I started to see the impact on the business side of things, and it'd never picked back up. I'd talked to customers, found the brands they really wanted and cut way back on the more expensive alcohol. I hadn't bothered to investigate bringing food back since that would've meant hiring someone else, and I couldn't handle another employee.

Not financially or personally, I thought as I looked at the paychecks I had to fill out. Aside from Gilly, my employees gave me a headache at least once a week. Some more than that. I tapped Ariene's name with my finger. I'd regretted hiring her by her second shift, and while she toed the line, she never crossed it enough to give me grounds to fire her.

Was it wrong that I was hoping she'd screw up so I could get rid of her?

I closed my eyes and rubbed my temples. Maybe she'd surprise me and end up turning around.

I'm too sexy–

I grabbed my phone just so I wouldn't have to listen to the rest of that song. I was pretty sure that was why Billy had programmed it as his text and ringtones. Well, that and the fact that he loved to walk around singing that damn song like he was some sort of male model.

Good looking? Yes, even though he had a bit of a baby face. He was on the short side but had nice broad shoulders and solid muscles. Well, muscles that used to be solid. Lately, he'd been drinking more and exercising less, so he was starting to get a bit soft, but I'd never thought of myself as being focused on looks.

hey babe gonna have 2 cancel 2nite srry

His abbreviations and his lack of punctuation drove me

nuts, but no matter how often I asked him to at least start separating sentences, nothing changed.

Is everything okay?

I reminded myself not to jump to any conclusions. He might've been flaking on me recently, but he'd been there for me when it mattered. He'd dropped everything when I called him to tell him that I was on my way to the hospital with my dad. He'd stayed with me while the doctors worked on Dad, and he'd held me when I'd gotten the news that the heart attack had been fatal.

So what if he'd canceled plans for the third time in a row? So what if we hadn't spent more than a few minutes together in weeks?

nuthin wrong mom needs me raccoon in the attic

I blinked, thinking I had to have read that wrong. His mother had a raccoon in her attic? A normal person would have called animal control – and that was exactly what I should have told Billy to do – but Mrs. Outhwaite wasn't exactly normal. She wasn't my biggest fan, even after all this time, convinced that I was going to steal her son away from her, so Billy and I spent as little time as possible with her. That didn't mean he'd blow her off when she was worried.

Call animal control. I typed anyway. *It could have rabies.*

My message changed from 'delivered' to 'read' after just a couple seconds, but no three dots popped up telling me he was responding. I set the phone down and stood, stretching my arms above my head. He'd been planning to come by and help me open the bar, then we'd go get something to eat. The weekdays were slow enough that I could take a couple hours off, especially when I'd been working my ass off. Now, I wouldn't be leaving, and I'd be opening by myself.

I twisted to stretch the muscles in my back and reminded myself that there was a rogue raccoon in Mrs. Outhwaite's attic. She needed Billy more than I did.

As I glanced down at my phone, however, I wondered if I really did need him at all. Hell, half the time, I barely noticed he wasn't there until he showed up.

I picked up my cleaning supplies and then headed out to the bar. Whoever was closing with me usually did the clean-up stuff that couldn't wait until the next morning – bathrooms, dishes, the usual bar dirty work – which meant I could do a wipe down and clean the floors on my own before we opened. I'd been doing it since I was a kid, so it was almost automatic anymore.

Giving me plenty of time to think while I worked.

Unfortunately, with Billy's text on my mind, that was what I thought about. How it wasn't actually too bad doing this myself, especially since Billy never seemed to help as much as I thought he would. He'd inevitably find something random – also known as easy – to do, like arranging shot glasses or double-checking the inventory I'd done twice already. Sometimes, he'd sit on the bar and tell me all about the ideas he had for the future.

Ideas that rarely ever included me or my bar, now that I thought about it. Then again, Billy's dreams were always unrealistic. Winning the lottery so he could buy the Celtics. Or some agent would spot him somewhere and offer him a movie role. After all, Tom Cruise was only an inch taller than he was. Or he could be an underwear model. A stuntman. A YouTube sensation. Those were some of his favorites, but sometimes he reached even further and talked about some idea he was sure could be sold on a show like *Shark Tank* for millions. Except his ideas were usually things like beer-scented cologne or dissolvable condoms.

Maybe that was why he never talked about our relationship or the bar; he didn't need to dream for any of that. But that didn't explain why he never talked about what the two of us were doing in those far-fetched daydreams of his.

Not that I'd ever call them that to his face.

I glanced at my phone again and saw he still hadn't responded. He was probably already at his mom's place because if he was on the bus, he would've texted back. Unless he was in the middle of watching something on his phone. Apparently, he'd been binging *Game of Thrones* the last three times he'd gone hours without responding.

More like watching all the sex scenes over and over.

I shook my head and went back to cleaning off the last table. People didn't understand why Billy and I didn't live together or why I wasn't pushing for an engagement, but the fact that I was more relieved than annoyed that he'd canceled yet again was proof that I was making the right decision to keep things the way they were.

I went back into the breakroom and put the paychecks in their usual basket, Gilly's on top since she was coming in first. She'd want to know why Billy and I weren't going out, and I'd have to tell her about the raccoon. I could almost quote every comment she'd make.

He's playing you, Syll. When are you going to realize that the two of you should have split years ago? Or even better, not dated at all. You're too good for him. Why are you staying with him? You can do so much better.

Gilly hadn't liked Billy from moment one, and things hadn't improved over the years. If anything, she was more critical of him, talking about him jumping from job to job, the way he apparently took me for granted, how often he borrowed money from me, especially when business was bad.

The knock at the door made me jump, but I welcomed the distraction. That was what I got for not turning on some music or something to keep all this shit out of my head.

I grabbed a towel as I walked to the door. It was almost time to open anyway. It was probably just a regular with a fast watch or something. Maybe it was Billy, coming by after he'd saved his mother from her furry intruder.

I hoped not. A burst of guilt followed my thought. I mentally cringed as I opened the door, unable to stop myself from still feeling like I preferred for him to not be there.

It wasn't Billy.

It was a middle-aged, average-looking man in a decent suit. He was the sort of guy who blended into a crowd, someone I could have met a hundred times and still not recognized.

"Good afternoon, Miss Reeve." Even his voice was average. "My name is Mr. Jones, and I represent an anonymous client who wishes to purchase your bar."

A thousand questions and comments flew through my head, but there was only one thing for me to actually say.

"No way in hell."

FIVE
JAX

I hadn't understood why Grandfather wanted me to come straight from the airport to work until I walked into my office and saw him sitting at my desk, going over printed copies of the contracts I'd emailed him earlier that week. I'd managed to get the company to go green, but he still preferred to read the paper version of things rather than digital ones. He said recycling was green too.

I supposed he deserved a couple quirks in his old age.

I walked over to my desk but didn't ask for my seat back. I could stand while we talked. I took a sip of coffee and then began giving him the rundown of how our New York office was doing. We'd been doing this for so long that it was almost second nature to rattle off the statistics I'd read through again on the flight home. He leaned back in my chair and held his hands in front of him, his fingers touching, mouth pursed in what I'd always thought of as his 'thinking' face. He wasn't looking at me, but I knew he was hearing every word.

He always did.

When I finished, I fell silent and let him take everything in. I might've technically been running the company, but as long as

Grandfather's mind was sharp, and he was interested, he'd be involved in any important decision-making. He was still majority shareholder.

"I'm assuming that you're satisfied, then, with the executives and their vision for the new year?"

I put my hands in my pockets and leaned on the chair. "I am. They were prepared, but not so much so that it made me think they were hiding something. No strange firings, or accusations from employees. They're hard working and expect a lot of their employees, but they also reward them."

"Excellent."

I took a deep breath. Even while I'd been reviewing information on the plane, I had this idea in the back of my head. I was drunk when I first thought of it, but it wouldn't go away. Not until I'd examined it, fleshed it out, considered it from all angles. If it wasn't feasible, then I could put it aside, but until then, it'd be like one of those annoying songs that got stuck in your head.

"Have you ever considered branching the company out to building businesses in addition to taking them apart?"

He raised one eyebrow, an annoying ability that I'd inherited but didn't like directed at me. "Was this a topic of discussion at the meeting yesterday?"

I shook my head. "Just something I've been thinking about recently."

"Building a business is a much different animal than dismantling it."

I swallowed a curse and a sigh. Grandfather had his *lecturing* tone. There was no point in trying to counter anything he was going to say or even responding until he was done with whatever knowledge he wanted to impart.

"The company we have is virtually recession proof, as long as we do our homework," he continued. "We control how things are broken up and resold. If no one's looking to buy something that's mostly intact, then we cut it up into parts people *are* willing to purchase. Sell the equipment for a call center as a whole, or sell off each computer, each headset, piece by piece."

I nodded in agreement. I'd heard that speech so many times I could quote it, but Grandfather knew that. Something else had to be on his mind.

"When you're starting a business, you can do all the research you want, but little things can come into play before you can even think. A turn in popularity. A bad review. Why risk it if what we're doing still works?"

He honestly wanted to know, but a part of me still felt like a little kid getting a lesson in Running the Family Business 101. "I saw a club in New York that was doing well and thought it might be an untapped market here."

"Boston doesn't need another club."

He wasn't being dismissive, but I knew that he considered the matter closed. He couldn't see the point, and unless I brought him hard proof to contradict what he was thinking, he wasn't going to waste his time with it.

"Besides, we have another project we should be looking at." He stood, picking up a set of rolled-up papers.

He carried them over to the low coffee table that sat in front of the small loveseat in the corner. I watched as he unrolled them, and then walked over to see what he had in mind.

"One of my contacts at the city planner's office sent me a tip this morning."

And now I understood why he'd insisted on us meeting this morning at the office rather than me giving him a brief summary of the trip whenever I happened to see him at home. This wasn't about our New York office at all. It was about whatever plan he'd hatched.

"There's going to be some changes made soon, and the prices of the property in this neighborhood are going to shoot up." He glanced up at me, and then traced a space on the city map. "If we can obtain any of the businesses here, the property alone will make us a considerable profit."

The reasoning was sound, of course, and I didn't doubt his information was good. He'd built this company by himself, not even having my father to help him back when he was alive. Dad's interest had only ever been in journalism. I'd seen, even as a child, how much it hurt Grandfather to not be passing down his company from father to son. After Dad died, I'd known that Grandfather would be looking to me, so I'd gone along with it. I had a knack for it, at least.

I studied the map carefully, taking in not only the area but the specific businesses that were already there. It wasn't in the best part of the city, but it wasn't in the worst either. With whatever the city had planned, I didn't doubt things would improve there, so it would make sense to invest.

I tried to get my focus on what Grandfather wanted, but as soon as I saw what sat on the corner, I knew it would be perfect for what I envisioned.

A single story but with high ceilings. Zoned for business. It was large enough that I doubted the entire thing was a bar. The back was probably storage since there was no basement. It'd be easy enough, though, to make it all one open space.

Perfect for my own BDSM club.

SIX
SYLL

Today officially sucked.

My bartender quit. Again. He was the third one in six months. At first, I thought it was because they kept finding places that paid more, but something about the way Stefan sounded when he called in to tell me he was leaving made me think that something else was going on. I asked if he could give me two weeks, but like the others, he said no. When I threatened the first two with withholding a reference letter, they hadn't said anything other than goodbye. Stefan, however, had said something about it not being worth waiting.

I didn't like to think it, but a part of me wondered if it was possible that Mr. Jones from earlier had also paid visits to some of my employees, giving them an 'incentive' to leave. Gilly hadn't mentioned that as a possibility, but I wasn't sure that meant anything. Not that I worried about her quitting. If she hadn't left yet, I doubted anything short of a natural disaster would make her go somewhere else. I didn't know, however, if she would feel like she needed to protect me from the knowledge that someone was trying to buy my employees out from under me.

Then again, maybe it was nothing. After all, if someone really was going after my waitresses, I supposed Ariene would have quit already, and she hadn't done that.

She'd just called in sick.

As I climbed into the shower, I reminded myself that I told my employees to call off if they were sick because I didn't want them spreading anything around. It was a good thing that Ariene had.

I probably could've convinced myself of that if I hadn't had Gilly's voice buzzing in my ear most of the night. As I shampooed my hair, the worst of it came parading through my mind, no better the second time through.

"I'M JUST SAYING, Syll, it's suspicious."

I glared at Gilly across the bar. "You think everything Billy does is suspicious. If he'd canceled his plans and Ariene had come in to work, you'd think he was fucking Stefan."

She tilted her head like she was considering the possibilities. "If I thought there was any chance that your boyfriend was gay, sure, I'd think that was a possibility, but he doesn't have enough fashion sense to be gay."

"You do realize that's offensive on about ten levels, right?"

She grinned at me as she whirled off with a tray of glasses. Considering she was the only one waiting on customers tonight, she was in a damn good mood. It was one of the first times I'd ever been glad that we were half-empty. Then again, Gilly would get to keep all of tonight's tips, so maybe she did have a reason to smile after all.

As she came back for her next round, she picked up like she'd never left.

"All I'm saying is that it seems strange that Billy's mom has a raccoon in her attic in January. Don't those things hibernate? I mean, okay, maybe it was hibernating in her attic, but then it should be sleeping, right?"

I gave her a look. "Do I look like I know anything about the wintering habits of raccoons?"

She shrugged and danced away again.

If I hadn't been the only person manning the bar and the cash register, I might've gotten on my phone to check, no matter how much I tried to tell myself that she was only riling me up to keep my mind off how shitty things were going tonight.

"Come on, Gilly," I spoke first this time. "You know as well as I do that Billy's mom is fucking nuts. She could be hearing a mouse and think it's a raccoon. Hell, she could be imagining the whole thing, or even flat-out lying about it. We both know she can't stand me."

"True," Gilly admitted. She'd been my sounding board more than once when Billy's mom had pulled this sort of thing before. "But this isn't the first time he's canceled plans."

"Everyone cancels plans," I countered. "Look, Billy and I have been together for a long time. I'm not going to mess up a good thing by accusing him of cheating on me just because he happened to cancel plans when one of my waitresses called in sick."

She leaned across the bar and put her hand on my arm, her expression sobering. "Syll, I love you, but you're smarter than this. You know that this isn't the only time you've had questions, and don't tell me that you don't have them now. I can see them on your face."

"Gilly."

"What about a few weeks ago, when he came over, and you smelled another woman's perfume?"

"He accidentally grabbed women's shampoo at the store," I said. "And before you tell me that's lame, he brought me the bottle."

"Two days later."

I sighed. "We have work to do and only two of us to do it. Why don't we table you tearing down my boyfriend for another time? We both know this won't be the last time you'll find something wrong with what Billy does."

I MUTTERED curses under my breath as I toweled off. I'd hoped that a hot shower would clear my head, but it hadn't. I was exhausted, but I had a bad feeling I wasn't going to be getting to sleep anytime soon.

Two hours later, as I stared up at the ceiling, I cursed the fact that I was right and started thinking of ways to get back at Gilly for filling my head with so much shit. At some point, I must've fallen asleep, because the next thing I knew, that damn alarm clock was going off again.

I had the strangest sense of déjà vu as I went through my usual morning routine, but that wasn't really anything new. In fact, feeling déjà vu was part of what made me feel like I was repeating things. The idea alone was enough to give me a headache, but after how badly I slept last night, I already had one.

Since yesterday had been so sparse, and I'd already set out everyone's paychecks – I had one less now, which was a sort of upside to being left in the lurch, I guessed – I didn't really need to balance my books. Just the thought of looking at numbers made my head hurt worse, but I knew I needed to get the work done. I'd been doing this long enough that I knew where I could slack off and where I couldn't. Bookkeeping was definitely a *no slacking* zone.

It took me twice as long as usual to get through everything, but since there was less of it, I finished in about the same time. With less to clean up, I was able to take my time and still get done with minutes to spare. Not that I had anyone rushing to get inside. This wasn't the sort of place where people lined up, eager to be first in line. Yesterday's knock at the door had been a fluke.

Except there was someone knocking at my door again.

I grabbed my broom as I crossed the room. Mr. Jones was going to get something a hell of a lot less polite than a *no* to take back to his employer. One time, I wouldn't shoot the messenger, but guys who didn't take *no* for an answer were destined to get a broomstick up their–

Everything I was going to say fell right out of my head as soon as I yanked the door open and saw who was standing there.

Sandy brown hair that'd probably never seen anything less than a two-hundred-dollar haircut. Intelligent pale blue eyes. Long legs, a trim waist with a muscled enough torso to make him lean rather than skinny. A strong jaw and features rugged enough to completely eliminate any possibility of him being called a pretty boy.

Well, *damn*.

"Hello." He gave me a charming smile that showed off teeth so straight and white that they must've paid for a dentist's new car. "My name is Jax Hunter."

I knew that name but couldn't figure out why. My brain didn't seem to be working at the moment. Shaking his hand just made it worse. I could feel the strength in his grip, but he didn't try to crush my hand like he had a point to prove, and I suddenly wondered what it would be like to have those hands touching other parts of me.

It was that thought that finally got my brain working again. I had a boyfriend. I couldn't think like that. Not even if I had Gilly's voice in the back of my head telling me that Billy checked out other women all the time.

I couldn't even argue with that point because I'd seen it myself.

Rather than trying to confront my wayward thoughts, I

turned all my attention to getting Jax Hunter out of my bar as quickly as possible.

"Why are you here, Mr. Hunter?" While probably better than a *what do you want* question, that wasn't exactly the politest way to start a conversation. Still, it was the best he was going to get at this moment.

"I'm interested in buying this bar."

My grip tightened on my broom.

Was he fucking kidding me?

SEVEN
JAX

I LIKED TO THINK THAT NOT MUCH COULD CATCH ME OFF guard, but that's where I was now.

Yesterday, after Grandfather had gone home with his maps and plans, I hadn't been able to stop thinking about that prime piece of real estate that would be perfect for a club. Grandfather wanted the company to buy up as many quality businesses in this area as possible, which meant it wasn't outside of his vision for me to investigate the bar. The fact that I was thinking about buying it myself for my own venture...well, I kept that detail to myself. Usually, Grandfather and I were in sync about these things, but this time, my gut told me to go for it.

Which was why I'd had my assistant, Blossom, get me as much information as possible on the bar. I liked going into things well-informed.

She'd given me lists of the property's owners as far back as she could go in a single day, as well as any articles that mentioned it. She had a bit more on the man who'd converted the former diner into the bar that stood there now. Inspection papers stated that Gareth Reeve, a Boston native, had converted the back half of the building into an apartment of sorts.

A police report from about ten years ago had been filed by Gareth for some minor vandalism on Halloween. The kids who'd done it had been caught, but Reeve had struck a deal where they worked off the cost of what they'd destroyed rather than sending them into the system. The next article mentioning him had been an obituary, listing a daughter – Syll Reeve – as his only living relative. A few legal papers followed, the gist of them being that Syll had inherited the bar from her father. Everything indicated that she still lived on the property, but business didn't seem to be going as well now as it had been.

A daughter who'd been passed down her father's dream meant that she'd view the bar in one of two ways. First, as a burden she'd been forced into taking and couldn't ever get rid of without major guilt. Or she'd think of it as honoring her father's memory and not even think twice about what she wanted for her life.

Either way, she wasn't going to be an easy sell.

All of that I'd known going in. What I hadn't been prepared for was the short, curvy brunette who was currently glaring up at me like I'd said something majorly offensive rather than just having introduced myself and stated my honest intentions.

She barely looked old enough to drink, but I felt confident in my guess that she was Syll Reeve. The place was still closed, and she looked far too annoyed to merely be an employee.

"Miss Reeve?" I gave her my most charming smile as I tried again. "Would it be possible for me to come inside so we can discuss a few things?"

"I don't think that's necessary." She gave me a once-over, but instead of the attraction I usually saw in women, her expression remained irritated.

I wasn't going to be as easily put off as that. "I don't think you understand, Miss Reeve. I've come prepared to negotiate. You haven't even heard my first offer."

She crossed her arms, pushing up a set of amazing breasts. If this hadn't been a business transaction, I would've prepared a whole other sort of offer for her.

"It doesn't matter, Mr. Hunter. My bar's not for sale."

I'd heard that before, and I was certain that Syll was just as firm in her resolve as the other men who'd thought they wanted to keep their property, but in the end, they sold. She would too. Everyone had a price. People who said otherwise just hadn't been offered the right incentives.

"Let me at least give you my contact information and what I'm prepared to pay." I reached into my jacket and pulled out a business card.

She didn't take it. "Let me make this perfectly clear, Mr. Hunter. This is my home and my business. I'm not interested in selling, especially to someone who spends more on a suit than my bar makes in a month."

And then she closed the door.

She actually shut the door on me. I couldn't believe it. No woman had ever done that to me. I'd had some people who were tough bargainers, ones who thought their properties were worth more than I was offering, but no one had been that downright rude.

Then again, it wasn't like I'd mentioned where I was from. Hunter was a common enough surname that she probably hadn't thought I'd come from Hunter Enterprises. Other people I spoke with knew the company I ran, understood that any offer I made was genuine, and most likely also knew that I had a reputation for being fair. Syll didn't know any of this.

I left, grateful I'd asked my town car to wait. Mid-January wasn't the time of year I wanted to be left standing on the sidewalk, waiting to find a cab. As I climbed into the backseat, I began to make plans for my next move. This was far from over. I needed to regroup and give her time to check me out. Once she knew who I was, things would go a lot more smoothly.

Except as my driver pulled into traffic, I realized that, from the moment Syll opened the door, my attention hadn't been on the bar. Sure, I'd said the words, and I did want the bar, but if I was being honest, I cared more about seeing what was under her clothes than finding out what the inside of the bar looked like.

I needed to get laid.

Between what happened at Club Privé, thinking about starting a BDSM club, and meeting Syll, my dick was furious at me. It'd been too long since I fucked someone, even just good, old-fashioned vanilla sex, let alone Dominating someone. Hell, I hadn't even jacked off in weeks. I'd been too tired, too focused on work.

I thanked the driver as he pulled up in front of my house, and then got back out into the Boston cold. For once, I was grateful for it. It was a hell of a lot easier than a cold shower. It wasn't as effective though. Or maybe it was just because the walk to the door was so short. Whatever the reason, I was still half-hard when I got inside.

I was partway up the stairs when I realized that I hadn't even intended to come home. I'd planned on going back to the office once I'd gotten a verbal agreement; so, I could make a pitch to Grandfather. With that specific property, I was confident he'd come around to my way of thinking. Instead, my head had been so full of Syll that I'd given my home address.

"Dammit," I muttered. It wasn't that I couldn't work from home, I just didn't do it often. I had to have a good reason, and those didn't crop up much.

I stepped into my bedroom and took off my tie and suit jacket. A glass of Highland Park would hit the spot even though I usually didn't drink this early. I untucked my shirt and undid a couple buttons as I poured myself a drink. There wasn't a point in driving all the way back to the office with only an hour or so left in the regular business day. I might as well enjoy my time at home.

I sat down in the overstuffed recliner opposite the bed. As I sipped my drink, I realized that I'd never considered all the possibilities this chair held. I didn't bring women to my house much, but when I did, we always stayed in the playroom. Which meant I'd never thought about the perfect view this chair had of my bed.

I wasn't a voyeur in the sense that I didn't want to watch my woman with someone else, but I did occasionally like to see a woman touching herself.

The woman who'd been haunting my thoughts appeared in my mind's eye. I could almost see her on the bed, naked save for a pair of red lace panties, her hands still as she waited for my command.

I shifted in the chair, unsnapping my pants as I let my imagination run. Syll's hands cupping her breasts, unable to completely hold them. Her fingers touching nipples the color of ripe peaches. Then one hand sliding down her stomach and beneath the waistband of her panties. Those full lips would part with a gasp as she stroked herself, the movement of her hand under the lace teasing me.

I freed my cock as I wondered what her pussy looked like. Did she shave? Go completely natural? Trimmed? A Brazilian? How soft would her skin be? I could almost taste her on my tongue.

My thoughts shifted to her mouth and the things she could do to me with it. Taste me. Lick me. Suck me.

"Fuck," I groaned as I fisted my cock. I could feel the pressure building quickly and knew I wouldn't last.

I was okay with that. I didn't usually fantasize about real women, and certainly not one I was trying to do business with, but I couldn't stop thinking about her. About what it would be like to feel those lips wrapped around me. Her hair brushing my thighs. Her hand cupping my balls, playing with them...

I came so suddenly that it caught me off-guard, and all I could think about was what it would be like to have her swallow me down, lick me clean, and...fuck. I was hard again.

EIGHT
SYLL

If I kept losing sleep like this, I was going to fall over at the bar. I was used to getting by with four to five hours of sleep and functioning without a problem. I'd done it through school, and I'd graduated in the top five of my class. If I'd wanted to go to college, I would've had scholarships, but money hadn't been the only reason I didn't go. Dad had needed me.

I'd worked my ass off right next to him, hadn't left a minute before he did, had woken up when he did. We'd worked seven days a week, as well as most holidays.

I knew how to function on very little sleep, but this was getting ridiculous.

We'd been a little fuller than normal last night, so even though Ariene had come in on her shift, I'd been kept busy. Too busy to think, but not too busy to miss Gilly's not-so-subtle comments about how much better Ariene must've been feeling. At least Ariene had stuck with flipping Gilly off instead of making a big deal about it.

Except a part of me found that more suspicious rather than less. Why hadn't Ariene asked Gilly what she was talking about? If it'd been me, I would've wanted to know what I was being accused of. And maybe it had been Gilly's constant nattering about the subject, but I could've sworn I'd seen guilt of some kind on Ariene's face. I supposed it could have been something as simple as the fact that she hadn't actually been sick, but Gilly had gotten into my head.

But none of that was what had kept me up last night.

No, all of that had been courtesy of Jax fucking Hunter.

Before the bar had started filling up, I'd done a quick internet search on Mr. Hunter since I'd recognized his name from somewhere. Of course, searching for a Hunter in Boston immediately brought up Hunter Enterprises, and then I remembered why I knew who he was. Jax was the grandson of Manfred Hunter, founder of Hunter Enterprises. They were among the richest families in the city.

No wonder he thought he could buy my bar.

Except it wasn't anger that had kept me awake either.

It'd been those pale blue eyes. That strong jaw. It'd been wondering if his mouth would be soft against mine, or hard and demanding.

I thought it'd be the second. Something about him had seemed...rough despite his polished appearance. Not the sort of rough that scared me, though maybe it should have. No, this was the kind of rough that made my stomach clench and my body tingle.

Billy was the only man I'd ever had sex with, and I'd never had such a visceral response to him.

But it hadn't been guilt keeping me up either.

It'd just been Jax. Thinking about his body, his hands...

I'd been so hot and bothered that I'd gotten up after a couple hours to take a cold shower, but it hadn't helped. Even when I'd finally fallen asleep, I'd dreamed about him, then woke up with the space between my legs throbbing.

I'd ended up taking a couple of those cold tablets that had some extra sleep aids in them, which was why I was now waking up at quarter past noon. Even after I saw the time, I couldn't muster up enough energy to get out of bed. My head was foggy enough that it took me nearly a full minute to remember *why* I should get up. And then it took me another minute to decide that I needed to do it.

By the time I managed to make it to my office, I knew that I wasn't going to be doing the books today. I'd be lucky if I could run the cash register. Hopefully, cleaning things up would give my head a chance to clear.

When I stepped through the door to the bar, for a moment, I thought I hadn't woken up yet after all. Because this had to be a nightmare. Or maybe one of those weird *Through the Looking Glass* kind of dreams. That would make sense out of what I was seeing.

The door was wide open, the glass window broken, shards on the floor. Tables were upside down or on their sides. Chairs too. A couple had chunks gouged out of them, but it didn't look like anything was broken. Well, not any of the tables and chairs anyway. I saw pieces of at least a dozen glasses, on both the ground and the bar.

Someone had trashed my bar.

I blinked and waited for it to disappear, but it didn't. Someone really *had* trashed my bar.

What the hell?

I took a few steps inside, glass crushing beneath my shoes. That's when I saw what else my vandals had left behind. A piece of paper, attached to my bar with a butcher knife.

I reached for it, then stopped. I wasn't sure if this was as sinister as it looked, or just a bunch of kids doing shit on a dare or for the hell of it, but until I'd decided whether I was going to call the cops, it'd be better if I didn't touch anything.

I leaned over so I could read what was written in big, blocky letters.

Get out. Or else.

Not the most original or subtle of messages, but it definitely got the point across.

I sighed and reached into my pocket for my cell phone. First, I called the police department, and then I took pictures of everything. No matter how tight money had been, I'd paid my insurance. They'd want pictures and documentation of everything.

Then I called Billy. I could feel the adrenaline rushing through my veins, and I knew once the cops were gone, everything would sink in, and I wouldn't want to be alone when that happened.

After the third ring, Billy's voicemail picked up. "Hey, someone trashed the bar. I know you're working right now, but I could really use you here." I paused, then ended the call when I couldn't think of anything else to say.

I supposed it was a good thing that he hadn't answered. It meant his job was going well. He'd only gotten the job at the deli yesterday, but I was hoping this one would work out, at least for a while. He hadn't been thrilled about it, but at least it paid a little over minimum wage, and it was only a few blocks away. It also looked like it was doing really well, which meant he wouldn't get laid off or let go to cut expenses again.

Shit. I hadn't thought about what it could do to his job if he took off to come be with me. I sent off a quick text and hoped he'd take the time to read it before calling.

Please just come by when you get off work. I could really use you here.

Then again, as the police pulled up in front of the bar, I wondered what, exactly, Billy would even do when he got here.

NINE
JAX

NORMALLY, IF SOMEONE I WANTED TO DO BUSINESS WITH had rejected an offer, I'd wait a couple days, give them a chance to think about things, then return with something new if they didn't contact me first. Sometimes, they called, wanting to accept my original offer because they realized it was the best they'd get.

Somehow, I didn't think that Syll would think that way. Which meant I should have been analyzing her business, coming up with a new approach since I hadn't even had the chance to tell her what I'd pay for her bar. Working on a Saturday was normal for me, but I couldn't get myself to focus on anything other than how much I wanted to see Syll again.

By late afternoon, I'd given up on concentrating on anything and decided to head over to her bar. I hadn't gotten a look inside last time, which meant I did have a legitimate reason to go there. Seeing Syll was just a bonus.

If it was really business, I should've put on a suit, and if it was just to see inside, I could've worn the same casual clothes I'd been in already. Instead, I chose a nice pair of jeans and a long-sleeved shirt that I'd always been told I looked good in. I didn't even bother to try to explain it away.

The moment I got out of the car, I realized something was wrong. The bar wasn't open yet. Or maybe it was. It was difficult to tell since there wasn't a sign on the door. Because there wasn't a door. More or less.

"Syll?" I didn't even try to hide the concern in my voice as I went inside. "Hello?"

"Hello?" She stepped out of the back room, a broom in hand. Her eyebrows shot up when she saw me. "It's you."

"What happened?" I gestured around me as I took in the chaos.

"Some asshole broke into my bar, trashed the place, and left a threatening note." She glared at me. "That's what happened."

A flash of anger went through me, and I took a step toward her. "Are you okay?"

Any decent guy would've asked the same question, but that didn't explain me wanting to find out who'd done this and kick his ass. And if he'd hurt her...my hands curled into fists at just the thought of it.

"I'm fine," she said, a bit of surprise in her voice. "But I can't say it makes me feel good that I was sleeping when this happened, and I didn't hear it."

I leaned down and picked up a tipped over table. "Did you call the police?"

"They left about five minutes ago."

"And they just left you by yourself?" I ran through a mental list of my contacts at the local police department, wondering who I could talk to about getting a squad car to watch over her... the bar. Watch over the *bar*.

"I am an adult, Mr. Hunter. I'm quite capable of taking care of myself." I had to admit, she sounded more pissed than scared. "Even when people aren't above trying to bully me into doing what they want."

I turned at the accusation in her voice. She'd set aside the broom and was now glaring at me, hands on hips.

"Are you trying to imply something?" I asked mildly.

She shook her head. "Not implying anything. I'm flat-out saying it. You came here, with your expensive suit, said you wanted to buy my bar, and when I said no, you acted like you hadn't heard a word I said. Like you had some *right* to keep talking when I said I wasn't interested."

Was she serious?

"I just think it's kind of funny that the day after I told you something you didn't want to hear, my place gets trashed and I got threatened."

"I would never–" The sentence broke off the moment I realized what she'd said. "You were *threatened*?"

"The cops took the note and the knife–"

"The *what*?" I took another step toward her, vaguely aware that I was getting into her personal space.

"I'm fine," she said, holding her ground. "But I still think it's a little suspicious that this happened right after I turned down two of your offers to buy my bar."

It finally hit me then. She thought *I* had done this. Trashed her place. Threatened her.

"I don't know what you've heard about me, or what you think you know about me," I fought to keep my voice even, "but I would *never* resort to threats or vandalism because a deal didn't go through."

"How do I know I can trust you?" Her eyes met mine.

"I wouldn't hurt anyone," I insisted. "Least of all you."

"Least of all me?"

Shit. I hadn't meant to say that out loud. Hell, I hadn't meant to *feel* it. She was close enough now that I could smell her citrus shampoo. I wasn't going to try to explain to her what I meant because I didn't want to think about it. I did, however, want to see if she tasted as good as she smelled.

It would be so easy to reach out and touch her, to put one hand on her waist and pull her against me so I could feel how her body curved. My other hand tangling in those curls to hold her still while I took her mouth, explored every inch with my tongue.

She swallowed hard, her eyes wide. I had no doubt she could read on my face everything I was thinking, but she didn't step back, didn't tell me to keep my hands to myself. I gave her a minute to decide if she was going to stop me because, if she didn't, I'd kiss her and damn any consequences to my business venture.

Just before I acted on my desire, I heard crunching glass behind us.

I spun around, automatically putting myself between Syll and the stranger who was walking into the bar. He was short and stocky, with buzzed hair so pale that it had to be either a very light blond or premature gray. The arrogant light in his hazel eyes told me that he was sizing me up as competition of some kind, underestimating me, and most likely overestimating his own ability.

Even though I'd never set eyes on this guy in my life, I knew his type. Ones who carried chips on their shoulders and thought that the world owed them something. He was exactly the sort of man who'd do something like this, whether for revenge or for money. If he thought he could intimidate me, he–

"Hey, babe."

The glare he gave me was at odds with the easy tone of his voice and his word choice. Which meant he was talking to Syll. And calling her *babe*.

"I came as soon as I could," he continued, opening his arms as Syll stepped around me. He hugged her, shooting me a smug expression over her head. She pulled back enough to look up at him, and he kissed her.

I clenched my jaw tight and forced myself to keep my

expression blank. I didn't know Syll, and I sure as hell didn't have a claim on her. Which meant that there was no reason why watching her being kissed by that smarmy asshole should piss me off so badly.

"Thank you for coming," she said when he finally let her come up for air. Her face was flushed, but something about it told me that it was more from embarrassment than passion.

Or maybe I was just reading her completely wrong again. After all, I had thought that she wanted me to kiss her less than two minutes ago.

Then again, maybe she had wanted it, and I'd misjudged her character.

All of this flashed through my mind in the time it took for her to turn back toward me.

"Ja–Mr. Hunter, this is Billy Outhwaite, my boyfriend."

Boyfriend.

Right.

"Billy, this is Jax Hunter."

"What's he doing here?"

I shoved my hands into my pockets, so I wouldn't 'accidentally' punch this douche in his face. "I stopped by and saw what happened. I was helping her clean up."

"And how do you know her?" He stepped toward me, a mulish glint in his eyes.

"I offered to buy her bar yesterday." I hadn't done anything wrong, and I'd be damned if I let him make me feel like I had.

He looked down at Syll. "You didn't tell me that."

She lifted a shoulder. "I haven't talked to you since then."

I wondered if I was the only one who could hear the irritation in her voice.

"Well, I'm here now, so you don't need to be." He crossed his arms, puffing out his chest in what I was sure was supposed to be a threatening gesture.

Too bad for him that I had three younger brothers, all well

over six feet tall, and much more intimidating than him. If I didn't let them push me around, I sure as hell wasn't going to let this guy do it.

"I don't think that's your decision to make." Thanks to dealing with all sorts of people in my business, I'd learned how to keep my cool when talking to pretty much anyone, but Billy was pushing my limits.

"Listen here, asshole." He crossed the distance between us until only a few inches remained, but I didn't flinch or back away. "She's *my* girlfriend. *Mine*. You got that?"

For a moment, I thought he was going to poke me in the chest, and if that happened, I knew I'd snap and probably break his finger. I needed to calm down because escalating this wasn't going to be good for anyone involved.

But that didn't mean I was simply going to take his shit.

"Step. Back," I said through gritted teeth. "She was here by herself, and after what happened, I didn't think that was safe."

"She wasn't by herself. I'm here."

I didn't bother pointing out that being here now didn't mean she hadn't been alone when I arrived. He didn't seem like the sort to take to kindly to that kind of help.

"Now you are," Syll spoke up. "He came in, we talked. He picked up a table. Knock it off and help me clean up."

He didn't even look at her, but after a few seconds, he must have considered me sufficiently cowed, because he took a step back.

And then he sucker punched me right in the face.

TEN
SYLL

"What the fuck, Billy?!"

Jax had his hand to his face, muffling his curses as he took a step back. He wasn't retreating though. I could see in his eyes that he was thinking of his next move. If this turned into an all-out fight, my already-trashed bar was going to be destroyed, and Billy would get his ass kicked. I didn't doubt that for a minute.

Part of me wanted to let it happen because Billy had been out of line. Not to mention the fact that when he pulled this possessive bullshit, it didn't make me feel safe and protected. It made me feel like I was a piece of property. That I belonged to him, and no one else was going to get to play with his toys.

Not exactly how a girlfriend wanted to feel. Not this girlfriend, anyway.

"You heard him," Billy said, his face red.

"Yeah, I did." I stepped between him and Jax. "And absolutely nothing he said made him deserve a punch to the face."

I didn't mention the fact that, right before Billy arrived, I'd thought Jax was going to kiss me. It would only make things worse, and I didn't even really know that's what Jax had been thinking. He could've been staring at me like that because he was trying to figure out the best way to convince me to sell.

Sometimes, lying to myself was the only way to get through the day.

Besides, even if Jax *had* kissed me, that would've been for me to deal with, not Billy. Not unless I had needed his help. And Jax wasn't like that.

"I can't believe you're defending him," Billy said. His voice had taken on that whining tone that always set my teeth on edge. "You're *my* girlfriend! You should be on my side."

"That's enough," I said sharply. "You need to apologize and back off. Jax didn't do anything wrong."

"*Jax?*" Billy glowered at me now. "What happened to *Mr. Hunter?*"

I shook my head, my patience wearing thin. "Suck it up and apologize to him. You were in the wrong here."

Tension stretched in the silence as I waited to see what Billy would do. He'd never gotten violent with me, but I knew he had a temper. And a childish streak that could make him unpredictable at times. If he thought I was taking Jax's side over him, he could sulk and leave, or he could make matters worse.

"No fucking way."

Okay, so it was making matters worse.

"Can I get some ice?" Jax asked. He was holding the bridge of his nose, but I didn't see any blood, so I hoped that meant nothing was broken. "I have a meeting next week that I'd rather not have black eyes for."

He was taking this rather well. I took a step toward the kitchen, intending to get him what he asked for, but I didn't make it any further because Billy's hand closed on my upper arm.

"Don't."

I turned around, looking down at his hand, and then back up at him. "Let go of me."

His grip tightened, a stubborn look on his face. "I mean it, Syll. Don't."

I tried to pull my arm free, but his fingers dug in, and I made a pained noise.

"She said to let go." Jax was suddenly there, towering over us both. "I suggest you do it."

"Or what?" Billy said belligerently. "I can break your nose this time."

"I don't think so," Jax countered, his voice low and dangerous. "You're not going to catch me off-guard again. That was your one freebie."

"You know what, Billy," Syll sighed, "get out."

Both men looked at me, surprised, and I took the opportunity to pull my arm free. I took a couple steps back but didn't take my eyes off Billy. I pointed at him. "You need to leave. You're behaving like a child, and I've got enough to deal with right now. I can't handle this too."

"C'mon, Syll," Billy protested. "I'm your boyfriend, and you're going to kick *me* out?"

"You're the one causing the problems," I said. "Leave."

"Say the word," Jax said quietly, "and I'll make him go."

For a moment, I worried that, rather than preventing a fight, I was provoking one, but then Billy scowled and looked away. "Fine."

I waited until he left before looking over at Jax. My annoyance shifted from my boyfriend to this near-stranger as I saw him looking far too pleased with himself. "And what the hell were you thinking? Provoking him like that?"

His eyes widened. "*I* provoked *him*? Do I have to remind you that he punched me in the face for no reason?"

"I don't know about that," I said. "He came in here and saw a strange man in a trashed bar with his girlfriend. For all he knew, you'd done that to get to me."

Jax shook his head, but he looked amused more than angry. "You don't really believe that, do you?"

I pushed back sweat-dampened curls from my face and sighed. "I believe that I'm tired of men talking over me and around me."

"That's not what I was doing," he said. "I was trying to protect you."

"Protect me? He's my boyfriend. I was never in any danger from him."

"I think the bruises you're going to have on your arm would say otherwise."

I glared up at him, all my previous thoughts about how gorgeous he was disappearing as I realized how annoying he was. "I had it under control."

"Yeah, you did."

I reached out and poked him in the chest, then tried not to show how surprised I was at just how hard his chest was. "You don't know me. I don't care how much research you did on me and my family before you came in with your offer, but that doesn't mean you know shit about who I am, or what I'm capable of."

He held up his hands in the universal *I surrender* gesture. "Hey, I didn't mean anything by it."

"I'm just saying that I can fight my own battles. I always have."

Something in his face softened. "But you shouldn't have to."

No. I didn't want him to say something like that. I didn't want him to look at me like he wanted to protect me. I didn't need that from anyone. I never had. My father had raised me to be tough, to think for myself. I knew he hadn't wanted to leave me so young, but he'd always meant for me to be able to look after myself when he was gone. He'd never trusted Billy to do it.

And I was starting to think that I never had either.

"Don't get cute," I said quietly. "Billy's my boyfriend. Yeah, he was out of line, both with you and with me, but what would you have thought if you'd been in his position?"

He was silent for a minute, considering the question before answering it. "Did you call him as soon as you saw this?"

"Right after I called the cops." I narrowed. "What does that have to do with anything?"

"The cops have been here and left again," he said. "I didn't see any of them, so I'm guessing they were gone about five to ten minutes before I got here. But he was completely calm and relaxed when he got in here. Acting like it was okay that it took him all this time to get here."

"He was at work." Even as I defended him, I couldn't help but remember how frustrated I'd been when he hadn't answered his phone.

Jax moved into my personal space with one step, his expression serious, his eyes darkening. "No work, no person – *nothing in this life* – would have kept me from getting to the woman I loved if I thought she was in trouble."

Oh.

Then he was cupping my face and lowering his head.

His mouth was firm against mine, nothing timid or hesitant about it. His lips moved, parting mine so he could trace my mouth with the tip of his tongue. His teeth scraped against my bottom lip, and I made a sound I'd never made before.

It startled me enough to make me realize what he was doing. To *really* realize it.

I pushed him away, intending to simply tell him never to do it again, but then I saw the smirk on his face, and my temper got the best of me.

I slapped him.

ELEVEN
JAX

It had just been a kiss.

A fucking *kiss*.

I'd had my first kiss in sixth grade. Katie Paladino. A seventh-grade volleyball player. I'd been the envy of every boy in the sixth and seventh grades, and probably some in the eighth grade too.

Remembering my first kiss wasn't weird. Most people remembered that.

A single kiss that took less than a full minute, and had happened a few hours ago, should not have still been on my mind.

Then again, it could have been because I could still feel my cheek stinging from where she slapped me.

I wasn't mad at her for it. I'd crossed a line. Before I'd known that she had a boyfriend, it hadn't been too far-fetched to think that she'd want me to kiss her. Once I found out about Billy the asshole, I should have backed off. But then he grabbed her arm, and I'd seen red.

But I still shouldn't have kissed her.

Bad, bad, bad idea.

Especially considering I'd been half-hard ever since.

So, I was heading to The Estate to see if I could find someone to take to a hotel and work off some sexual tension. Someone who was *not* a short, curvy brunette.

Having Syll still on my mind was why, as soon as I entered the club, I started looking for someone who wouldn't remind me of her at all. I'd come here a few times over the years. The music wasn't bad, but I never stayed to dance. That wasn't why I was there.

I scanned the crowd, waiting for someone to catch my eye, but I kept dismissing each woman I saw. It was Saturday night, so it wasn't like my selection was limited. I just kept finding different reasons why I didn't want to approach woman after woman.

"You look like you know what you're here for."

I turned toward the female voice. She was tall, her heels putting her at nearly six feet, and her little red dress showed off her slender body. Beautiful features and smooth, caramel-colored skin. She was a knock-out, no question.

"What do you think I'm looking for?" I asked, interested for the first time in someone since I'd walked into the club.

She took a few steps toward me before answering. "I think you're looking for me."

I let my gaze slide down her body, and then back up again. The Dominant in me preferred someone a bit more submissive, but I wasn't looking for a partner, just a fuck.

"And why do you think I'm looking for you?"

She stepped right up to me and put her mouth by my ear. "Because I've spent the last two hours waiting for a guy like you to come in and fuck me."

"A guy like me?"

"A man who will follow me to the bathroom and fuck me so hard that I'll feel it the rest of the night. The kind of fucking that a bad girl like me deserves."

I put my hand on her hip and squeezed, watching her face for any sign that she didn't want a bit of pain with her pleasure. I was more about control and Domination than about sadism, but I also liked being rough, so I always needed to make sure that my partner was aware of that fact as well.

"I'm not looking for a relationship," I said.

"I don't even want to know your name," she countered with a smile.

"Then we're on the same page."

I took her hand and pulled her after me as I made my way through the crowd. This was better than I could've hoped for. I'd been fully prepared to buy drinks, rent a hotel room, make small talk. Now, it looked like I was going to get what I needed without all the extra crap that went with it.

I liked The Estate because it was one of the classiest clubs in the city, but that didn't mean people didn't still have sex in the bathrooms. She locked the door behind us a few seconds before I had her up against the door.

I kissed her hard, my hands pulling up her dress even as she worked on getting my pants open. I growled against her mouth as she wrapped a hand around my cock, stroking me with short, rough jerks.

I let her have a couple tugs before I stepped back and turned her around until she was facing the door. I didn't want to look in her eyes while we fucked. Too much intimacy. Hell, I wouldn't have even kissed her if I hadn't been trying to get the taste and feel of Syll off my lips.

I shoved my hand between her legs, and she moved them apart to give me better access. Her thong was soaked, but I didn't really take that as much of a compliment. She could've been turned on for some other reason. I'd come here with someone else on my mind, after all.

It would make things easier though.

I slid a finger inside her, and she cursed, pushing back against me. "I don't need much foreplay."

I shoved a second finger into her, and she yelped. "Trust me." I almost called her *babe*, but then I heard in my head another voice using that same endearment and decided against it. "Trust me," I said again. "I'm a bit too big to go without any foreplay."

"I've heard that before." Her voice was breathless as I worked my fingers in and out of her.

I pulled my fingers out and reached into my pocket for a condom. As I rolled it over my shaft, I said, "Well, you'll feel it in a moment."

She threw a sultry glance over my shoulder. "Promises, promises."

I didn't bother to answer. The banter should have been sexually charged, but it wasn't really doing it for me. Not that it mattered. The best part about hooking up like this was that there'd be no hurt feelings from either one of us if we didn't pretend. I'd get her off, and she'd get me off, and we'd both leave here happy.

I pulled aside her thong with one finger, then used my other hand to position myself. I'd take her hard and fast, but I always had to start slow, unless I was playing with a sub who was into pain, and even then, I didn't do it often. I eased the head of my cock inside, and she moaned.

"Damn, you weren't kidding." She was panting after only a couple inches, then cursing when she realized I wasn't all the way in.

Finally, I bottomed out and held myself there, giving her a moment. I reached between her and the door, covering one of her breasts with my hand. Her nipple was hard against my palm, telling me she wasn't wearing a bra. I pinched it, pulled on it until she started squirming. Then I started moving, driving into her with the sort of punishing strokes that were all about reaching climax as quickly as possible. The hand on her breast moved down her front until I could slide my fingers against her clit. I alternated motions until I found the one that made her shiver.

Listening to her talk about how good I made her feel should've been turning me on, but all I wanted to do was tell her to be quiet because I wasn't here to have my ego stroked, and the more she talked, the less I was into this.

And the more I kept wondering if Syll talked this much during sex. And if it would bother me as much as listening to this nameless stranger did. But if it did, I could always see how much she could talk with my cock in her mouth.

Fuck if that didn't make me harder than all the shit Miss Anonymous was saying.

I could see it perfectly. Syll on her knees, those soft lips wrapped around me. Olive eyes looking up from under her lashes. Silky waves between my fingers. Throat contracting around me as I came...

I came then, taking Miss Anonymous with me a few seconds later. I was glad I'd been able to get her off, but I'd been done with this since before it was over.

What the fuck had that woman done to me?

TWELVE
SYLL

Why the hell couldn't I stop thinking about that kiss?

I hadn't asked him to kiss me. I hadn't *wanted* him to kiss me. So, if I thought about it at all, I should've been angry. But I wasn't. All I could think about was how I'd felt in those few fleeting moments before common sense kicked in and I'd pushed him away.

How right it had felt.

The worst part was, I couldn't really think of anything to distract me. I'd cleaned the bar up by myself. I'd tried opening for the night and then sat there alone, waiting for customers. Or for Billy. Or for anyone. No one had come, not even Gilly. That wasn't really her fault, though, since it was her night off and I hadn't told her about the break-in. So, no matter what thoughts I tried to use, they all sucked, and that just made me feel worse.

Now, it was midnight, and I should've been preparing to close things down, but there wasn't anything to do. No tables to clean, no glasses to put away. Nothing to keep me from locking myself in my office and crying.

Things had never been easy for me growing up, but I had no

regrets about my childhood. Sure, it would've been nice to have been one of those kids who came to school after Christmas break bragging about the gaming system they got or one of those girls who'd gone to some elite boutique to buy her prom dress, but I wouldn't have traded my father's love for any of it.

His death had almost broken me, but I'd gotten through it because I'd known that's what he would've expected. He'd raised me to be independent, to stand on my own two feet, to make my own choices. I just hadn't planned on needing to do it so young.

Even when I'd been grieving over him, I'd always had in the back of my head that I could do this. I could keep his dream alive, make this bar into a tribute of sorts to him. I'd keep it in the family, pass it down to my own kids. We'd all work here together. Dad had never said that was what he wanted, but it was how I could keep him alive for me.

Despite the financial difficulties I'd had in the two years I'd been running this place myself, I'd never once allowed myself to think that I couldn't do it. Not until now.

I sat in my office with the door open; so I could see out into the bar. I hadn't locked the front door yet, but I couldn't take sitting out there alone anymore. I wasn't afraid of the vandal coming back, not even after their bit of theatrics with the knife, but it was too depressing. At least, this way, I could pretend that I was working and keeping an eye on the place; like I'd done many times in the past when I'd had a full crew working.

I hadn't talked to the insurance company yet, but I had my list of things that needed to be replaced, and a note to go down to the police station to get a copy of the incident report. There wasn't really anything else I could do. I couldn't even start shopping until I knew how much the insurance would even cover.

I was still wallowing when I heard the front door open. A flash of unexpected fear cut through me, adrenaline dumping into my system and getting me to my feet. I reached for the baseball bat that had sat above the desk, hoping my muscle memory was good enough to let me swing the bat like I had growing up. I'd hit my first home run with it, and maybe it still had a bit of that luck.

"Syll?"

I sagged with relief. "Back here."

I put the bat back in its place but didn't sit down. A moment later, Billy came through the door, and I launched myself at him. I was still pissed about his previous behavior, but that could wait until my heart went back to its normal rhythm.

"Are you okay?" he asked.

"I'm still a bit shaken after what happened earlier," I admitted. "I'm glad you're here."

"Yeah, well, I didn't like how we left things," he said. His arms tightened around me. "I shouldn't have lost my temper. That guy just got under my skin is all."

I knew that was as close to an apology as I was going to get. Him even admitting that he was wrong was something, and I was too tired to push for anything more.

"You know I love you, babe." He loosened his embrace, so I could look up at him. "Are we okay?"

I nodded. "Thank you for coming back."

He gave me the charming, rakish smile that had gotten my attention back in high school.

"You're my girl," he said. "What kind of man would I be if I didn't make sure you knew that?"

He bent his head and touched his lips to mine. I closed my eyes, trying to lose myself in the familiarity of his kiss, to let it wash away any remnants of the kiss Jax had given me.

Then Billy's hands slid from the small of my back to my ass, and I knew he wanted more than a kiss. He had a pattern when he wanted sex. First, he'd kiss me, then he'd grab my ass. Then came the sweet talk.

"You're so fucking hot, you know that?" He kissed me again, as if to punctuate his statement.

His tongue slid between my lips, moving back and forth like he didn't have any real goal in mind beyond having his tongue in my mouth. Unless I slowed him down, he always kissed like that, but tonight I didn't care about slow. It was okay that he wasn't a great kisser because that wasn't what was important. He was here with me, and I desperately needed to feel that I wasn't alone.

When he came up for air, I focused on getting his pants undone. If he was inside me, we'd be here together, in this moment. Nothing that happened before would matter because he'd be with me.

"You have an amazing ass." He slid his hands under my shirt and unhooked my bra before pulling everything over my head. "And amazing tits."

I opened my desk drawer, feeling around for the emergency condom I always kept on hand. Some people might think it strange to have an emergency condom in their work desk, but if they had a boyfriend who constantly forgot to buy them, it was important.

"Really, babe? We couldn't go raw just one time?" He fondled my breasts, squeezing them like they were a pair of stress balls. "You're on the pill."

I nodded and wondered if it was worth it to ask Billy to take it easy on my breasts, maybe put in some time playing with my nipples. No, I wasn't in the mood to coach foreplay. "I am, but you know we always double up. We're not even close to being ready for kids."

He gave me a sad look, the sort of pouty, puppy-dog-eyes expression that had always tugged at my heartstrings. Now, it just annoyed me. I'd told him a hundred times my reasoning for still using condoms.

I shoved my hand down the front of his pants, under the

waistband of his underwear, and wrapped my hand around his erection.

"Fuck." His eyes closed as I gave him a couple firm strokes. "You're so good at that. It's almost as good as being in your mouth."

I rolled my eyes at his not-so-subtle hint. If I went down on him, he'd probably go in my mouth, and then not return the favor. While that wasn't a problem at times, tonight, I needed his attention to be on me rather than himself. I pushed his jeans and underwear down enough to free his cock, then rolled the condom over him.

"Since this is make-up sex and all, what do you think about doing something different?"

I looked up at him as I pulled down my own pants and underwear. "Different?"

He grinned and turned me around. My hands came down on the edge of my desk, knocking aside a stack of bills. His hands were on my breasts again, and his cock was hard as it rubbed against my thigh.

"After all these years, we should spice things up, don't you think?" He kissed the back of my neck, then grabbed my ass, kneading my cheeks. "You said we'd talk about it, and I think tonight would be a great night to do it."

It took me a moment to realize what he was talking about. I glared at him over my shoulder. "Are you kidding me? You want to fuck my ass *here*? Like this?"

He shrugged. "It'll be fun."

"Yeah, for you maybe, but I don't have any lube here. Plus, that's not exactly the sort of thing you do as a quickie."

Irritation flashed across his face, then disappeared. "Fine."

For a moment, I wondered if he'd try to do it anyway, but then I felt the head of his dick at the right entrance and I relaxed. It was crazy to think Billy would force himself on me.

He just didn't get how something like that really worked. Planning wasn't exactly his strong suit.

"Tell me you want it, babe," he said as he pushed inside me. "Tell me you want my cock in your twat. Do you want me to fuck you like a little whore? Say it. Say you're my good little slut. My slutty little bitch."

"Dammit, Billy, knock it off." I was starting to think it'd be better just to take a shower and go to bed. "You know I don't like that."

Dirty talk was one thing, and if someone else liked to be called a whore and bitch, hey, that was their choice, but I didn't, and Billy damn well knew it. We were going to have to have a talk again about how what he saw in porn wasn't what I wanted.

That was something for another time though. Right now, I closed my eyes and focused on the familiar feel of him sliding in and out. I wanted him to make me come, for us to be in this together. A woman's orgasm had mental components as much as physical ones, and I knew if I was in the right mental state, it would be a lot easier for him to coax one from me.

"You're so fucking hot," he groaned. "I'm so close."

Already? Dammit.

I reached down between my legs, wishing I could ask him to do something besides grabbing my breasts, but I knew from experience that he didn't take guidance in the bedroom well. My fingers found my clit with the sort of practiced ease I didn't like to think about too much. I rubbed the little bundle of nerves back and forth, trying to catch up to Billy, but I knew from his rhythm that he wasn't going to last much longer.

"Fuck!" he shouted as he came.

I sighed and waited for him to pull out. He wouldn't stay the night, not since he'd gotten off already, and after he left, I'd finish things off myself. I still needed the stress relief after what happened today, but if I asked Billy to help me with that, he'd start on how it wasn't his fault that I couldn't climax with him, and it'd just make things worse.

Then, a whisper echoed in the back of my mind. *If Jax can kiss like that, who knows what else his mouth can do.*

Dammit.

I was back to that damn kiss again.

THIRTEEN
JAX

"Harder, Sir, please fuck me harder."

"Whose pussy is this? If you tell me whose pussy this is, I'll fuck you harder. I'll make you come so hard you'll see stars. Tell me."

"Yours! It's yours, Sir. Please fuck me hard–"

A shrill ringing cut through my dream and jolted me awake. I had a moment to realize that I hadn't been dreaming about my encounter with Miss Anonymous, but rather something completely different...with Syll Reeve, and then I answered the phone.

"Yes?"

"Jax, this is Germaine."

It took me a moment to place the name, partly because she'd only rarely ever called me by my first name, and never used her own first name. It was that more than the fact that she was calling so late that cleared the last of the sleep from my mind.

"I'm your grandfather's attorney."

"I know who you are, Ms. K." I hoped I didn't sound as rude as I felt, but it was midnight. "I'm guessing it's something urgent that had you waking me up, so let's dispense with the small talk and get straight to the point."

"Your grandfather is in the hospital."

I blinked. I had to have heard that wrong. I'd just seen him. "What?"

"Manfred – Mr. Hunter – was just taken to the hospital in an ambulance. You need to come right away."

"I'm on my way."

It didn't occur to me to ask how she knew Grandfather had been taken away in an ambulance since I lived in the same house as him and hadn't heard anything, but it wouldn't have made a difference anyway. The important thing was that I needed to get there, and I dressed with an urgency I'd never felt before.

Not that it was serious. It couldn't be. Grandfather was the healthiest person I knew. He ate right, didn't smoke, didn't drink to excess, exercised as best he could at his age, and had regular check-ups. Hell, he was hardly ever even sick. He wasn't one of those old people who had to get flu shots and wear masks in public. My whole life, I could count on one hand the number of times I'd seen him sick enough to call off work, and I couldn't recall a single time he'd been in the hospital.

Which meant this was just a false alarm. He'd eaten something that didn't agree with him, and Ms. K had panicked. Or maybe he'd fallen, and she wanted to make sure he didn't break a bone.

Except Ms. K didn't panic. I'd met her on more than one occasion and had been struck by how calm and intimidating she was. I wouldn't have ever wanted to be on the opposite side of a case as her. So, the fact that she seemed so freaked out bothered me.

Not too much, though, because Grandfather was fine.

He was always fine. Always there. He'd been there to take in my brothers and me after our parents and sister died. He raised us by himself after Grandma Olive had passed, and that was no easy feat. He was tough. He could handle anything life threw at him.

I kept reassuring myself the entire ride to the hospital, but it did little to calm the mass of worry settling in my stomach. Once inside, I was directed to a waiting room where I saw Ms. K pacing. Her severely cut gray-and-blonde hair was a mess, her clothes wrinkled, and she was wearing a path in the floor.

"Ms. K," I said as soon as I was close enough to get her attention.

"Jax." She came toward me, and for a moment, I thought she might hug me. "Manfred was at my house this evening, and he passed out. I couldn't get him to wake up, so I called 911."

This evening? It was past midnight.

How had I not known that Grandfather was seeing Ms. K?

That was just one of the many questions I'd ask him when he was better. Because he would be better.

"Where is he?"

She gestured toward a pair of double doors. "I told them I was his attorney, so they've given me a couple updates, but any medical decisions that need to be made, that has to be done by you."

Medical decisions? What sort of decisions was she talking about? Grandfather had fainted. That's all. Maybe he was dehydrated.

"He woke up," she continued, "but he was disoriented. They've been running tests."

I awkwardly patted her shoulder. "Thank you for calling me. If you want to stay, you're welcome to, but if you want to go home, that's fine too."

She nodded and went back to pacing, and I went over to one of the chairs to sit. Because sitting showed I wasn't concerned. Because he was going to be okay.

I wasn't sure how much time had passed when a tall, thin

woman in purple scrubs came toward us. I jumped to my feet, ready to hear that I could go back and see Grandfather while she started the discharge paperwork. He wouldn't want to stay here any longer than absolutely necessary.

"Are you Mr. Hunter's grandson?" she asked.

"Jax Hunter." I held out a hand, and she shook it. "Can I see him?"

"I'm Dr. Kassum. I was called down to consult on his case. I'll take you back to see him shortly, but you need to know how serious his condition is before that."

Serious? That didn't make sense.

"Your grandfather suffered a severe heart-attack."

Okay, that *was* more serious than I'd thought. But people survived heart-attacks every day, especially if they were otherwise healthy. He'd get through this and be home by the end of the week at the latest.

"The damage to his heart was...catastrophic."

Ice flooded my veins. "What do you mean *catastrophic*?"

"His heart is damaged beyond repair. It's failing."

That couldn't be right.

"We've made him comfortable, but you should call in any other family you have."

"What about a transplant?" I demanded. "Artificial valves, that sort of thing. There's things you can try."

She shook her head. "I'm sorry, Mr. Hunter, but there's not. At his age, with his rare blood type, the chances of finding a heart quickly enough is a million to one. And even if we did find one, the chances of him surviving surgery are less than ten percent."

I heard a small sound behind me and knew that Ms. K was crying. I couldn't comfort her though. How could I make her feel better about something I couldn't understand? This had to be a mistake. I could get a second opinion. Ms. K could threaten legal action. We had options.

"I explained this to your grandfather, and he declined being put on the transplant list. He said he wants us to keep him alive until his grandsons arrived, and then he wants no more heroic measures."

All the strength ran out of my legs, but I didn't collapse. I couldn't. I had to be strong. For my brothers. For Grandfather. I wouldn't let him down.

"Excuse me," I said quietly. "I have calls to make."

FOURTEEN
SYLL

It was always cold when I came here, but I preferred it that way. Even if the sun was out, the cold kept things bleak, and I wanted them bleak.

"I tried," I whispered as I reached out to touch the stone. I could feel the chill even through my gloves, but the external temperature had little to do with what I felt all through me.

The marker was small, but I hadn't been able to afford anything else. Not without selling the bar and making myself homeless in the process. Dad wouldn't have wanted that. In fact, he probably would have laughed at me for wanting anything here at all. We'd never been the sentimental type. Or, at least, I'd tried not to be.

Gareth Bradley Reeve Age 47 Beloved Father

It wasn't nearly enough. Those seven words didn't say how he'd been a single dad from the time I was three. Or how he'd taught me to ride my bike in the bar, so he could keep an eye on me while he did the paperwork. It didn't let everyone who walked by know that he'd gone without new shoes, so I could have a prom dress.

I drew in a shuddering breath and wondered if I'd ever be able to come here without feeling like my world was ending all over again. I missed him so badly that it hurt. I had Gilly, but I didn't know if she would always be there. I didn't know if whatever had sent her to Boston years ago would send her away.

"I don't know what to do, Dad." I straightened but kept looking down at the marker. "I've tried to keep things going, but I don't think I can anymore."

Movement out of the corner of my eye caught my attention, and I glanced toward it, expecting to see someone with flowers, or maybe a few stones, to lay at a grave. Instead, I saw Mr. Jones.

"Not here," I said, shaking my head. "You don't do this here."

He held up a hand. "Please, Miss Reeve, hear me out." I glared at him but made a gesture for him to continue. He did. "You need to stay away from Jax Hunter."

Okay, not what I'd been expecting. "I don't understand."

Mr. Jones gave me one of those patronizing looks that men his age gave women of all ages who dared to question them. "I think you do, Miss Reeve. You need to stay away from Mr. Hunter."

"I have a boyfriend." Heat rushed to my cheeks as I realized the statement wasn't necessarily about the kiss. Mr. Jones had an employer who wanted my bar, after all. "And I told you I wasn't selling."

He gave a half-shrug. "Everyone knows that being in a relationship doesn't necessarily mean anything."

The way he said it made me think it wasn't just some sort of off-the-cuff remark, no matter how casual he sounded, but this wasn't a conversation I wanted to be having. Not here, not with him.

"Look," I said, "you need to leave. Whatever message you have for me, you can give it to me any other time or place. Just not here."

His eyes darted down to the stone at my feet, but there was no apology on his face when he looked back at me. "My instructions were to come here and tell you to–"

"I know, I know, 'stay away from Jax,'" I said. My temper was simmering now, and the last of my patience was gone. "You do realize that whatever asshole you're delivering your message for sent you to find me at my father's grave, on the anniversary of his death?"

He didn't even have the decency to look embarrassed, and that just pissed me off more.

"I have a message for you to take back to your boss. I might've considered selling at some point in the far future, but they crossed a line sending you here today. I'll see my bar burned to the ground before I'll sell to them. You go back and tell them that they fucked up."

I couldn't tell if he was ignoring me, or trying not to laugh, but I meant every word of what I said. I didn't like being told what to do, but I could've overlooked the strange 'warning' if Mr. Jones had just come to the bar. This would've been too far even if I hadn't just had the shittiest week ever.

"I admire your determination, Miss Reeve, but let me assure you that once my employer sets their sights on something, they don't stop until they get what they want. I recommend that you do as you've been told and avoid Mr. Hunter." He smoothed back his slick hair. "I'm sure I'll be seeing you soon."

I couldn't think of anything to say to any of that. I had a feeling that he was telling the truth, both about his employer and about me seeing him again. I wasn't sure, however, what he'd meant by the relationship comment. Unless, of course, he'd seen Jax kiss me, and then left before he saw my response. But that wasn't any of his business.

And neither was my relationship with Jax. My non-relationship. Because he and I didn't have one.

And we never would.

At least that was one less thing I had to worry about with Mr. Jones' employer.

FIFTEEN
JAX

For the last twelve hours, I'd been alternating pacing in the waiting room, the hallway, and my grandfather's room. I would've loved to go outside and get some air that didn't stink of disinfectant and illness, but the doctor's words kept echoing in my head, and with them came a host of memories I didn't want.

I'd been eight when the accident happened. Like Cai and Slade, I'd been with friends, and we'd stayed there while Grandfather had taken care of things. It hadn't been until years later that I learned what happened that night. That my dad hadn't been killed right away like Mom and Aimee but had been unconscious when he reached the hospital. He and Blake had both been taken to the hospital. Dad had never woken up, but Grandfather had still seen him.

I hadn't. In fact, my last memory of the family I'd lost that night had been me getting reprimanded for teasing the twins. I'd never seen my parents or sister again. They'd been cremated, their ashes placed in the family vault. The funeral had been formal, completely planned by my grandparents. They'd been so worried about what we'd lost, they hadn't asked us if we'd wanted to see our parents one last time, so we could say goodbye.

As much as I struggled with resenting my grandfather for not giving me the opportunity to see my dad one last time, I didn't want the same thing to happen with him. I planned on being here until the end.

"Is there anything else you need?"

Blossom's voice pulled me out of the past, and I was grateful for it. This was bad, but that was worse.

"No, thank you, Blossom." I gave her a polite smile. "This is good for now, but I may need you to run things back and forth until..."

I let my voice trail off, unable to say it yet.

She reached over and put her hand on my arm. "Whatever you need, I'm here for you. No matter when you need me."

"Thank you."

She didn't ask if I was thanking her for the offer, or for bringing me my work laptop and files, and I was glad because I honestly didn't know how I would've answered that. But I was still glad she was there. I didn't have many people in my life I could count on, and with her, I always knew where I stood.

I went back into Grandfather's room and took the uncomfortable seat in the corner. He was sleeping again, or rather, still. He'd been awake for about ten minutes the first time I'd seen him, but since then, every time I'd come into the room, he'd been out.

I could barely look at him, which made me even more grateful that I had something to do. Except I couldn't concentrate. I'd start to read a sentence, then get distracted by his heart monitor. Or how still he was laying. Or how old he looked.

Or the fact that he was never going to leave that bed.

And that was always when I started looking at my phone to see if I had any messages from my brothers. As tense as things were sure to be between us, it'd be better than sitting here by myself.

It was well into mid-afternoon when I heard someone enter the room. It'd been three years since I'd last seen him, but I recognized the sound of his footsteps. Cai and I were thirteen months apart in age, and I didn't have a single childhood memory that didn't have him in it.

I looked up, and for a moment, the child I'd known and the man he'd become overlapped. The golden blond hair and bright blue eyes were the same. Cai had always been tall, but his freshman year of college, he'd gone from matching me at six feet, two inches, to passing me up by three inches, making him the tallest of us four.

"Jax." His voice was still as calm and even as always.

I'd always loved trying to make him mad when we were growing up, but I'd rarely ever managed it.

"Cai." I stood and quickly crossed the space between us. I held out a hand, and we had a moment of awkward hug-or-shake before he shook my hand. "Thanks for getting here so quickly."

"I wouldn't have if you hadn't had a private plane ready for me." He shrugged off the bag he was carrying and walked over to the bed. "What happened?"

"His heart." I stuck my hands in my pockets and went to stand next to Cai. "We had a meeting Thursday afternoon, and he was fine."

My brother gave me a sharp look, and I prepared myself for the reprimand.

"Don't you live in the same house?"

I rubbed my forehead, but it didn't make a difference to the headache I'd had almost since I'd first gotten here. "You know how huge that house is, and how independent he is. Do you think he'd tolerate me keeping tabs on him?"

Cai didn't respond, but he didn't need to. I already knew the list I'd get from my brothers of how I'd fucked up.

"It came out of nowhere," I said. "Dr. Kassum said there was nothing in Grandfather's medical history that could've predicted this."

A moment of awkward silence fell, and I tried to figure out something I could say. Things hadn't always been easy between us, but after the accident, Cai had disappeared on me. I'd needed his help with Slade and Blake, but he'd gone off and done his own thing. He was still doing that. He was questioning how often I'd seen Grandfather, but Cai hadn't even been back to Boston in three years. I was the one who'd stayed, who'd taken over the family business.

"How's business?" Cai asked, almost as if he'd known where my thoughts had gone.

"Good," I said. It was on the tip of my tongue to tell him about my ideas for a club, but I held back. He was just being polite. He'd never cared about Hunter Enterprises. Hell, I didn't think he even cared about his dividend check. "How's work?"

He shrugged. "Dealing with epidemics isn't exactly as glamorous as traveling around on the company jet."

I gritted my teeth. He had to go there. I'd rented private planes for him and Blake, so I could send the company jet to pick up Slade in Texas. It hadn't been a slight. But that was Cai. Always picking at the way I did things.

"Well, we can't all be doctors." That came out a lot glibber than I'd meant it, but that was how it'd been between Cai and me for more than twenty years.

"Some things never change."

Grandfather's hoarse voice cut through the tension.

"You're awake." I tried not to let the relief bleed into my voice, but I wasn't sure I succeeded.

"Don't worry, Jax, I'll stick around until the rest of the boys get here." His eyes were calm as they met mine, and I wondered if he'd always known how I'd felt about not saying goodbye to my dad.

"I'd like to speak to your doctor," Cai said, squeezing his hand. "I want to make sure they've thought of all possible treatments. It's always good to have second opinions."

I wanted to remind him that his area of expertise was infectious diseases, which worked great at the CDC but wouldn't do shit for Grandfather's heart, but I kept my thoughts to myself. I wasn't about to waste what little time we had with Grandfather arguing with my brother.

"Dr. Kassum is one of the premier cardiac specialists in the country," Grandfather said.

I recognized the stubborn set of Cai's jaw because all of us Hunter men had it. He wasn't going to let it go.

"There's nothing more to be done."

And there was the voice of the Hunter patriarch. When he said things were finished, they were finished.

I just never imagined that he'd be talking about himself.

GRANDFATHER WAS SLEEPING AGAIN, and Cai had left, muttering something about coffee. I was certain he was going to try to hunt down Dr. Kassum, or one of the senior staff. Once he got something in his head, he didn't give up for anything. I wasn't going to try to talk him out of it though. A small part of me even hoped that he'd prove all of us wrong and come up with a solution that made all this worry and waiting for nothing.

But I didn't believe it would happen any more than I believed Grandfather would miraculously get better. I saw it in his eyes. He was done fighting.

"How is he?"

I pushed myself out of the chair as Slade and Blake came

into the room. Slade had texted me when he arrived, letting me know that Blake was only a few minutes behind him and that the two of them would be coming in together.

Of all of us, Slade was the only one who looked like Mom. He had her dark brown hair, easy smile, and a lot of the same features just morphed into something a bit more masculine. His eyes were the only thing of Dad he had, but his baby blues sparkled the same way Mom's always had when she laughed.

With a start, I realized that this year, he'd be the same age Mom had been when she died. I wondered if he knew it.

"He's been awake on and off," I said quietly. "But when he's awake, his mind's clear."

Slade nodded, his expression uncharacteristically serious. "You know, I think a part of me thought he'd outlive us all."

"I know what you mean," I said.

Of all my brothers, Slade was the easiest to get along with. Maybe that was why he'd chosen to move to Texas, so he wouldn't get caught in the middle like he had so often as a kid. It hadn't been fair of us to do that to him, especially me. I'd been the oldest, and I should've looked out for him more, but this wasn't the time or place to discuss old grievances and open old wounds.

I gave Slade a half-hug, trying to remember the last person I'd hugged before this, and I couldn't think of anyone. Blossom had done the sympathetic arm squeeze thing, and that was rare for her. It wasn't so much a professional thing with her as it was her personality. The women I slept with never hugged me. We kissed, fucked, and sometimes laid next to each other, but we didn't hug.

When I stepped back, I turned my attention to my youngest brother. We wouldn't hug. By the time he was ten, he'd declared that he was too old to be 'hugged like a baby' and that had been that. Like all of us, he had blue eyes and was tall, but he was muscular too, making him look even bigger. His light brown hair was scruffy, longer than when I'd last seen him, and he had at least three days' growth of a beard on his face. He looked more like someone we'd dragged from the mountains than part of one of Boston's most prominent families.

The sullen glower on his face didn't help matters much.

The circumstances being what they were, however, made me focus on what was important.

"I'm glad you guys made it."

The *in-time* part of my sentence hung in the air between us.

I stepped aside and let my brothers walk over to the bed while I hung back. I'd had my time, and it was now their turn.

Slade had been only five when our parents died, but he had a few memories of them. Blake had been four, but he didn't have any memories of anything before the accident. He'd been in the car, conscious and crying until the paramedics had arrived. We'd all lost our parents and a sister, but Aimee had been his twin, and they'd been inseparable.

This was going to be hard on all of us, but I suspected it would be the worst for Blake. We were losing our grandfather, but Blake was losing the closest thing to a father that he remembered. With our own relationships so...distant, I doubted Grandfather's death would bring us together. If anything, it would tear us even further apart. I needed to accept the fact that, barring a miracle, this would probably be the last time I saw my brothers, maybe ever.

SIXTEEN
SYLL

Today was all about getting back to normal. Because everything that'd happened in the past week had not been normal. Not at all. Not the part where a gorgeous billionaire kissed me after someone had trashed my bar and threatened me. Not the part where I couldn't stop thinking about him.

None of it.

But today, for three blissful hours, I was going to do something that had nothing to do with any of that. I would throw out dead flowers and water live ones, talk with those who didn't have anyone else, and offer assistance to families. I'd pour water and get ice chips, throw away trash. Basically, everything that was the glory of being a volunteer at a hospital, I would do.

This was the hospital where they'd brought my dad after his heart attack. He hadn't survived to make it to a room, but the doctor who'd told me that they'd done everything they could had found me a couple hours later, after Billy had gone home, and she'd sat with me. When I'd come back a few days later to thank her, she'd suggested that I look, into volunteering. A month later, I showed up, and I'd been doing the same two to three times a month ever since.

I pulled my hair back into a ponytail, grabbed my coat, and headed outside. It was colder today than it had been in a while, and I shivered as I walked down to the bus station. It hadn't snowed on Christmas, but the weather was calling for it today, and the gray, overcast sky told me it would be here soon.

I used to like the snow, especially when it was so deep that no one would come into the bar except the men who couldn't live without the booze. Even most of them had chosen to stick close to home rather than slog all the way down to our bar, no matter how much they might like it. That had meant Dad and I had the bar to ourselves, and a whole world of white outside.

Those sorts of days hadn't happened often, but when they had, we'd stay in and read, or go outside and make snowmen in the street, or maybe watch a movie and drink hot cocoa. I hadn't understood until I was older that days like that had cost us money, but even that hadn't been able to make me regret those wonderful memories.

I didn't like those days now. They meant sitting in an empty bar alone, trying to determine what I'd have to cut so I didn't lose the heat or electricity. They meant trying to keep things positive as I texted Gilly while also trying not to snap at Billy when he asked for phone sex.

Tonight, wasn't supposed to be that bad, but Monday nights were the slowest nights anyway, and I'd estimated that I'd spend more money trying to keep the place open than I would lose if I closed it tonight. So, I'd made the executive decision, and for the first time since my father's funeral, the bar was closed.

I shifted in my seat, earning a dirty look from the old woman sitting next to me. She'd been sniffing and clearing her throat from the moment I'd sat down, clutching her purse like I was going to steal it.

"Is there something I can do for you?" I asked, keeping my tone as sweet as possible.

"You're that Reeve girl, aren't you?"

"Do I know you?"

"I used to see you with your father at that bar. Distasteful, I used to say. Having a child at a bar. Won't come to any good."

I smiled. "You're right. I'm twenty-four years old, and I own my own business. No good at all." I stood up. "If you'll excuse me, I think I'll get off here."

The wind stung my face as soon as I stepped off the bus, but I kept walking. I was three blocks from the hospital, but I preferred the cold to sitting next to that woman for one more minute. She had no business talking about my father that way. I didn't know who she was, but I'd known plenty of people who'd thought the same way. I'd heard the whispers at school, and then the kids who hadn't even bothered to try to whisper.

I blamed the weather for the water freezing on my cheeks, and by the time I reached the hospital, I was ready to work and forget all about the fact that I'd been crying. I threw myself into every task the nurses set in front of me, desperate to have my mind focused on anything but my life.

I was so focused on *not* focusing on anything that I was a full foot past him before I recognized his scent.

Because that wasn't creepy.

I opened my mouth to say hello, but that was when I saw he wasn't alone. Jax stood just inside a room with three impressive-looking men who had to be related to him. Maybe brothers. He hadn't said anything about having brothers, but it wasn't like we'd really spent much time talking about anything other than my bar and my boyfriend.

Right, boyfriend. I needed to remember Billy and forget about Jax. It didn't matter why he was here unless someone asked me to look in on them. Considering I was essentially done, that wasn't going to happen. And that was a good thing.

I'd gone another foot or so down the hall when I heard a noise behind me and turned to see Jax disappearing around the corner.

I didn't even think about what to do. I just went after him, catching up at the elevators.

"Jax?"

He didn't look at me, but the muscle in his jaw clenched, and I knew he'd heard me. When the elevator doors opened, I followed him inside. His expression was stony, his eyes like ice. I couldn't feel the arrogance and swagger that I'd recognized in him each other time I'd spoken with him. I couldn't feel anything.

"Are you okay?"

He didn't speak, but the fists his hands had made kept opening and closing, like he couldn't quite stay still. Like there was something inside him filling him with a nervous energy that he needed to get rid of.

I reached out and put my hand on his arm. His muscles tensed under his shirt sleeve, but he didn't shake me off.

I repeated my question, "Are you okay?"

He shook his head. "No, I'm not."

The pain in those three words twisted my heart. "What can I do?"

The doors opened, and as he walked out, he said, "Nothing."

I shook my head. I wasn't going to let him go that easily. Something was wrong. It didn't matter that I slapped him the last time we'd seen each other. This was about helping someone in pain.

I caught up with him again just before he made it outside. I caught the sleeve of his coat, and he turned so quickly that I sucked in a breath.

"I said you can't do anything, Syll." His voice was low, thrumming with something primal and dark.

"Let me help you." I reached up and put my hand on his cheek. "What happened?"

"My grandfather died."

The grief I saw on his face hit close – too close – to what I'd gone through with my dad. All the feelings I'd been trying to work out of my head came rushing back, and all I wanted to do was take that pain from him because no one should have to feel like...

His mouth came down on mine hard and fast, and I could taste the desperation, the need. Not necessarily need for me, but for what I could offer him. Solace. Oblivion.

All the things I understood about wanting. So, I didn't push him away. I wrapped my arms around his neck and did what I wanted to do the first time.

I kissed him back.

SEVENTEEN
JAX

I couldn't stay in that room with the machine letting off that long, steady sound that meant he was gone. My brothers were adults. They didn't need me to stand with them the way I'd needed to when we lost Grandma Olive or our parents and sister. But I couldn't let them see how much I was hurting either. I needed to be alone.

When I heard her say my name, I'd almost told her to leave me the hell alone. But she'd asked if I was okay, and she'd meant it. Not because she was after my money or wanted something from me, but because she really wanted to know. I was honest when I told her there was nothing she could do, but when she hadn't let me go, something in me snapped.

And I kissed her.

Again.

But this time, she didn't push me away. This time, her arms were around my neck and her lips parted under mine. This time, I buried a hand in her hair, put the other on the small of her back, and poured everything I was feeling into her.

And for each one of those blissful seconds, I wasn't thinking about anything except the way her body felt pressed against mine, the taste of her on my tongue.

I wanted her.

No, more than that. I *needed* her.

She was the only person I could let see me this way. She wouldn't hold it against me, wouldn't think less of me for the pain I was in. She had no preconceived notions of who I was, and she didn't want anything from me. I didn't need to worry about us being splashed across the tabloids or her coming to me for money. This could just be about me forgetting.

I heard a sound behind me and realized that we were still standing in front of the doors. I didn't want to stop kissing Syll though. Once I did, I wasn't sure she'd let me do it again, and I *really* needed to keep doing it. I wrapped my arms around her and spun us around, so we were tucked into a small alcove behind a potted palm tree.

She made a surprised sound but didn't push me away. Her fingers dug into my hair, her teeth nipping at my lips before her tongue slid across mine. I pushed my knee between her thighs, rocking against her until she gasped. That was the spot. She squirmed, but I held her in place.

There were so many parts of my life that I couldn't control, and today had been the worst in a long time. But this, with her, was something I could control. Unless she told me to stop, I was going to make her come right here.

I pushed my leg against her harder, then bit her bottom lip, my entire body humming with a desperation I didn't fully understand. All I knew was that I'd never wanted a woman to come so badly before.

Her body tensed, and I knew she was fighting it. That just made me want it more.

"Let go," I murmured against her mouth before I took it again.

A shudder ran through her, and I swallowed any sounds she

would have made. My cock strained against my pants, and a part of me wanted to fuck her right here.

And then I remembered that *here* was the hospital where my grandfather had just died.

I ended the kiss but didn't pull away from her. I rested my forehead against hers, our mingled breathing sounding harsh in the relative seclusion of our little corner.

"I don't want to go home," I said, raising my head so I could look at her face. Her cheeks were flushed, pupils dilated, and her lips swollen.

Fuck.

"Jax."

Her voice was low, husky, and a bolt of desire so sharp it was almost painful went through me.

"I don't want to be alone."

Her eyes met mine, and I waited for her to make her decision. I probably could have coaxed her, guilted her, but I didn't want to do that. I wanted her to choose to be with me. Tonight. Just tonight.

"I closed the bar tonight," she said. "The weather's supposed to be bad."

I brushed my lips across hers. "Sounds like the perfect night to stay in." I started to straighten, then stopped as she grabbed my arms. "Are you okay?" I asked.

"My legs need a moment," she said wryly. Her blush deepened, and my cock throbbed as I imagined that color spreading across the rest of her skin.

"Here." I helped her over to a chair. "Where's your coat?"

I WAS WORRIED that when I came back downstairs with Syll's coat, the heat between us would've cooled enough for her to think twice about her offer, but all that happened was that she'd taken her coat and held out a hand to me.

I called my car service when I'd been going for her coat, so the town car was waiting when we walked outside. That burst of cold and swirl of snow that greeted us when we stepped outside made me grateful I'd thought ahead.

We didn't talk on the ride over to the bar, and the only place we touched was our hands. It was strange. The nervous energy that had consumed me for the past day and a half was gone, but it hadn't left behind the exhaustion that I usually felt after I'd been running on adrenaline for more than a day. Instead, I felt...grounded.

I didn't understand it, but I wasn't going to pick it apart either. For once in my life, I was just going to go with it.

"My place isn't going to be anything like what you're used to," she said as we entered the bar and headed for the back.

I could hear the nerves in her voice and squeezed her hand. "Thank you for letting me be here."

She nodded as she took off her boots and coat. "Do you want something to drink? I have beer, water, and some orange juice."

I stepped up behind her and wrapped my arm around her waist. "I'm not thirsty."

She turned and pushed herself up on her tiptoes to kiss my chin. "Me either."

I picked her up, cutting the height difference so I could kiss her as I walked her back to a worn overstuffed chair. I sat down, arranging her on my lap until she had a knee on either side of my legs.

Like this, we were the same height, and she looked in my eyes as she ran her fingers through my hair. I could see questions there, but she didn't ask any. This time, she initiated the kiss, and she didn't hold back.

I lost myself in her, my brain processing only the sensations of her and me and what we were doing.

She tasted like mint and chocolate – cocoa maybe – and I could catch the scent of it even under the smell of her shampoo. Her mouth was hot, lips soft, and they moved with mine in perfect rhythm.

Her curves fit perfectly against my hands, and I squeezed her ass before moving up under her shirt. Her skin was soft and hot under my palms, and as I moved to pull her shirt over her head, I waited for her to protest. Instead, she let me toss it aside, then moaned as I kissed my way down her chest. Her head fell back, hair brushing against the back of my hands as I nipped and licked the exposed skin just above the black cotton of her bra.

"Fuck, Syll, I can't wait to see you come again."

I didn't know if it was what I said, or the fact that I'd spoken, but whatever it was made her freeze.

"I'm sorry." Her voice cracked, and she scrambled off my lap. "I'm sorry, Jax, I shouldn't have – I have a boyfriend."

A pitcher of ice water wouldn't have killed my libido more. "Excuse me?"

"You know that," she said as she bent over and picked up her shirt. "He punched you in the face, remember?"

"Yeah, I remember." I stood. "But I figured you'd ended things with him. Because why in the *fuck* would you have done any of this if you were still with him?"

"I'm sorry," she said again. She looked miserable, but I refused to feel any sympathy for her.

I shook my head. "I'll see myself out."

EIGHTEEN
SYLL

I WAS NO STRANGER TO PEOPLE TRYING TO MAKE ME FEEL shitty about myself. Like that woman on the bus. She hadn't even been close to the only person who'd questioned my father's ability to parent. My mother had left when I was three. We had no money, and I wore thrift store clothes. I hadn't gone to college. All the things that people had thrown at me over the years had never made me think less of myself.

What I'd just done...

I covered my face with my hands as I sank down onto the chair. It was still warm from Jax's body heat, and his scent lingered even if he was long gone.

My stomach churned, and I couldn't even muster up any pity. I didn't deserve pity. I'd brought this on myself. I'd gone after Jax, telling myself it had been for the most innocent of purposes: to make sure he was okay. I could have let him go after he said I couldn't do anything. It wouldn't have made me a bad person. I could have walked away when he kissed me. Put a stop to it right away and told him that I wasn't interested.

But I hadn't done any of that. I hadn't even hesitated to say he could come back to my place when he said he didn't want to be alone. He had family at the hospital, and I'd asked him to come anyway. I'd seen them. He should've been with them instead of me.

The way he'd looked at me...my heart twisted painfully. I'd been so angry at him for trying to buy the bar and for kissing me, but none of that had even come close to the damage I'd done to him a few minutes ago.

Then there was the fact that I felt worse about what I'd done to Jax than I did about cheating on Billy. Sure, he'd been an ass lately, but he was my boyfriend, and he didn't deserve what I'd done. Just because I stopped things before we had sex didn't mean I hadn't cheated.

Cheated.

I bolted out of the chair, barely making it into the bathroom in time. I hadn't eaten much today, but what little I had came up. Even with my stomach empty, I didn't feel any better. I let out a gasping sort of sob and then retched again.

I had to come clean about what happened with Jax. It was the only way I could even begin to make things right with Billy.

But first, I needed to shower, to scrub away the memory of Jax's touch, of the way he'd made me feel. I couldn't think about any of that though. Billy was the one who mattered.

I SHIVERED the entire walk from the bar to the bus station but kept telling myself that if I hadn't crossed a line with Jax, I wouldn't have been outside when it started snowing. Billy's place wasn't far, at least, and if he didn't kick me out, I could stay there tonight. I knew I wasn't a perfect girlfriend, but I'd never done anything like this before, and I hoped that would mean something to Billy.

I could barely breathe by the time I reached his third-floor apartment, and very little of it had to do with climbing all those stairs. The elevator hadn't worked in this building since before Billy moved in. I wasn't going to complain today though. Whatever punishments the universe sought fit to dole out, I'd accept. I deserved every one of them.

I knocked on the door and waited. After half a minute, I knocked again.

"Pizza!"

I frowned, thinking I had to be hearing things. Maybe the woman across the hall had been waiting for a delivery and mistakenly thought I'd knocked on her door. The walls here were thin.

"The app says it's not here yet, Ari."

That was Billy's voice. I'd know it anywhere.

The door opened a moment later, and I felt like the wind had been knocked out of me.

Ariene Sward looked down at me with wide, startled eyes, and then she burst out into laughter.

"Oops."

The smell of alcohol would've told me she was drunk even if she hadn't been holding onto a bottle of whiskey. A bottle that I was certain had come from my bar.

It said something about me that I was angrier about the stolen alcohol than the fact that the half-buttoned shirt she wore – the *only* thing she wore – was Billy's.

"Billy-boy, we have a problem!" She kept looking at me as she called over her shoulder, that obnoxious smirk plastered on her face.

"Ari, what are you – shit."

I looked around her as Billy came into view. He wore a pair of faded boxers and white athletic socks, his usual post-sex clothing. I could see long, red scratches down his chest, and wondered, dispassionately, if he had matching ones on his back.

"Syll."

"I came over to tell you that I cheated on you." The words

came out evenly, surprising me. "I didn't fuck anyone like you obviously did, but I kissed him. And he made me come." Why I felt the need to add that last part, I didn't know.

A burst of giggles exploded from Ariene, but I kept looking at Billy. His face went red, and he stalked over to the door.

"What?"

"I kissed him." I paused, then corrected myself. "Actually, he kissed me, but I didn't stop him. And then I kissed him back."

"It was that asshole from the bar the other night, right?"

All my guilt was gone. "You do realize how hypocritical it is of you to be angry with me when you just finished fucking her, right? Because that's what you were doing before I got here. Fucking. And since you two have such cute little nicknames for each other, I'm guessing this isn't the first time."

Ariene snorted. "No, it's not the first time. We've been doing it behind your back for months."

I waited for the pain of betrayal, but it didn't come. I'd worked myself up about what'd happened with Jax, thinking of how unfair it was to Billy and how much my betrayal would hurt him. And the entire time, he'd been balls deep in Ariene.

Well, not the entire time. I knew from experience just how quick he was.

Without meaning to, I snickered.

"What's so funny?" Billy snapped.

My laugh was the crack in the wall keeping back everything I was feeling, and it all came rushing forward. To no real surprise, anger outweighed hurt.

"This," I said, "*this* is what's so funny. I came over here upset that I'd hurt you, and I might as well have stayed home for all you cared."

Billy's expression twisted into something ugly. "You can't blame me for this, Syll."

I shook my head. "For what I did? No, I can't, but you screwing around on me? Yeah, that's all on you."

He sneered at me. "It's not like you left me much of a choice. You couldn't expect me to be monogamous with someone who's so shitty in bed."

I stared at him. "Are you kidding me? Do you know how many times since we've been together that you've actually made me come during–" I stopped and shook my head. "No. There's no point in having this conversation. It's clear that neither one of us want to be in this relationship anymore."

"I should've dumped your ass years ago."

I shrugged. "Yeah, maybe you should have."

I left before either of us could say anything else, but I could still hear Ariene laughing behind me as I headed for the stairs.

Gilly was right, I thought as I walked back outside. She'd seen what I hadn't been able to – or maybe just what I hadn't wanted to. I'd tell her tomorrow. I wasn't in the mood for an *I told you so*, and I didn't think I'd be able to talk her out of doing something like breaking one of his windows. That sounded pretty good at the moment, especially since, the more I thought about it, the more my gut told me this hadn't even been Billy's first-time cheating. Sex was the same now as it'd been when we'd first started sleeping together, so if he thought it was so bad he needed to find it somewhere else...

I was suddenly even more glad that I'd always insisted on using a condom, and not only because I was grateful no kid had been caught in the middle of this. Who knew where his dick had been.

Maybe, deep down, I'd known all along that I couldn't trust him.

I needed a drink. Or two.

Maybe more.

NINETEEN
JAX

I looked down at my phone – again – and saw that Slade had called – again. I ignored the call and let it go to voicemail.

Again.

I didn't want to talk to my brothers. We didn't have anything we needed to say to each other now. Last night, Grandfather had told all of us that he'd made all the arrangements for his funeral years ago and had met with Ms. K regularly to keep everything up-to-date. Everything had already been paid for, and once he passed, all I would need to do is let Ms. K know, and she'd take care of everything else.

Which meant I didn't have anything I needed to do, including talk to my brothers.

I wished I had something to do. Anything to get my mind off how my horrible day had gotten even worse.

When I left Syll's place an hour or so ago, I automatically came back home. By the time I thought of going to the office, I was already home, and the snow had been coming down twice as hard. I knew that even if I did decide to brave the weather, I wouldn't have anything at work to do, and Hunter Enterprises had almost as many memories of Grandfather as the house did.

Besides, the only scotch I had at the office was for the occasional drink after closing a deal. It was good stuff, but I never indulged in drinking for pleasure, not even when I worked late or on a weekend. Drinking at home, however, wasn't a problem for me at all.

I'd taken a shower first though. I needed to get her scent off me. It'd driven me crazy the whole way home.

It hadn't helped.

I was currently sitting in front of one of my floor-to-ceiling windows, working my way through my third glass of scotch, and I still couldn't quit thinking about Syll.

If I closed my eyes, I could still taste her on my tongue, stronger than any alcohol. The first time I'd kissed her had been nothing compared to this afternoon. Hot and sweet, so eager. Then, watching her come on my leg...I could only imagine what it would be like to make her come on my mouth, on my cock. The sounds she would make. The things she would say...

"Fuck," I muttered as I thought about listening to her talk dirty. Keeping her on the edge of orgasm and not letting her come until she told me everything that she wanted me to do to her, all the secrets she was keeping.

I frowned as a sound cut through my little daydream. A dinging sound that it took me a moment to recognize. Someone was ringing my doorbell. I considered ignoring it, but then I remembered that my brothers were in town, and I doubted they still had their house keys.

Grumbling nonsense, I stood up and made my way downstairs, half-hoping they'd be gone by the time I got there. I wasn't in any mood for company.

"I'm sorry."

I processed the words before my brain recognized that the person in front of me wasn't one of my brothers. Syll was covered with snow, but I could still see her shivering as she peered up at me, looking as miserable as I felt.

"I was an asshole."

And she sounded like she'd been drinking a little too.

I stepped to the side and gestured for her to come inside. I shut the door behind her and then turned around, unsure what I was going to say to her.

I wasn't prepared, however, for her to launch herself at me. I caught her out of pure reflex, but I couldn't stop the groan as her body collided with mine. She pressed her lips against mine, the kiss sloppy and uncontrolled, but there was a hunger in it that I recognized all too well.

I took two steps back, then leaned down to set her feet on the floor. "What are you doing here?"

"Well," she blew out a sigh as she started to shake the snow off her coat. "I felt like coming to see you."

I raised an eyebrow. "And what does your boyfriend think about that?"

"Pfft." She scowled. "My *boyfriend's* an even bigger asshole than I am."

I reached out and took her hand, wincing at how icy her fingers were. "I don't like you calling yourself that."

"But I was," she insisted. "Kissing you when I was with Billy the asshole."

Her words weren't slurred, but she was definitely buzzed. I had a feeling she wouldn't have come here if she wasn't, but it didn't change the facts.

"Then why did you come here and kiss me again?" I asked. I found myself almost smiling as she almost fell over trying to take off her boot, then reminded myself that nothing had changed. "If that makes you an asshole like your boyfriend?"

She came over to me and tipped her head back, so she could meet my gaze. "I misspoke. He's my asshole *ex*-boyfriend."

I regarded her for a moment, and then asked, "Do you want to talk about it?"

She shook her head. "He's been fucking one of my waitresses for months. Nothing to talk about."

Ouch. "Want a drink?"

She shook her head again. "Already had one. Or three. Now I want to fuck."

Just when I'd thought my day couldn't get any weirder.

"Syll," I started.

She stepped closer and slid her hands under my shirt. My muscles twitched at the cold, but I didn't move. My nipples hardened as her fingers slid over them, and my blood rushed south.

"I'm not asking for anything but sex," she said. "I don't want to think about anything, and I don't think you do either. What do you say we help each other out?"

There was one thing I had to know before I answered, "Why me?"

"Because I like you," she said. "Even though I hate you for trying to buy my bar."

I wasn't even going to try to figure out that logic.

"You smell good, and you're hot." She ran her hands down my torso and then hooked her fingers into my waistband. "Plus, you made me come, and it's been a long while since someone besides me has done that."

That was good enough for me.

THE BED in the closest guestroom was only a queen, and it didn't have any of the little additions I'd made to several of the other beds in the house but getting her naked was more important than having all of my toys.

"Pants off, now," I said as I stripped off my jeans. Both of us had shed our shirts somewhere in the hall, and I drank in the sight of her bra-bound breasts again. "That off too."

She grinned at me as she shimmied out of her pants, her flesh jiggling delightfully. I'd never thought of myself as having a type, but after tonight...

I kicked my pants off to the side and wrapped my hand around my cock, watching her slip off her bra and reveal a pair of the most perfect tits I'd ever seen. I stroked myself slowly, blocking out everything except what I had in this room right now.

"Panties."

"You're bossy."

But she obeyed, and that was what was important.

"On all fours," I said when she was completely naked. "On the bed."

"I've got to warn you," she said as she climbed onto the bed. "I'm counting on you making me come again, and I've never come in this position."

I crossed to the bed and reached down to grab her hair, twisting it so that she was now looking at me over her shoulder, her eyes dark with desire. "I have two rules. One, if I do anything you don't like, you tell me."

"Okay."

"And two, I don't want to hear about the shitty lovers you've had in the past. Tonight, I'm going to make sure you forget your own name."

"That's what I'm hoping for," she said, her voice breathless. I tightened my hand, and she gasped but didn't protest. "Now, let's talk about your punishment."

"My what?"

The hand not tangled in her hair came down on her ass with a smack hard enough to make her yelp.

"I think you need to be punished for what happened before." I slapped her ass again. "Don't you think?"

She swallowed hard, telling me she was new at this, but she didn't tell me no, so I was going to take that as a positive. We wouldn't get into anything too extreme, but after the day I had, I couldn't promise I wouldn't get a little rough. I released her hair and spanked the other side of her ass just to even things out. Then I squeezed her ass and pulled her cheeks apart. She sucked in air as I slid my thumb down her crease and stopped at the puckered ring of muscle. I brushed over it, letting her catch her breath again.

"Not tonight," I said softly. I wasn't even sure why I said it, because tonight was all we had talked about. Still, the thought of taking her ass was one that made me wonder if maybe this didn't have to be the only time.

I slid my hands around her hips, up her ribcage, and palmed her breasts. My cock slid between her ass cheeks as I pinched her nipples between my fingers, tightening my grip until she shivered. I straightened then, smacking her ass again with one hand, and reaching into a bedside drawer with the other. I ripped open the wrapper with my teeth and then rolled the condom on.

"Now," I said, "let's see if I can't get you off like this."

TWENTY
SYLL

Jax got me off twice, pounding into me from behind, one hand in my hair and the other slapping my ass until it burned.

And he hadn't come yet.

How the hell did he have this much stamina?

My muscles were still trembling as he leaned over me and worried my earlobe between his teeth. "What do you want to try next? I'm thinking I want you riding me, so I can watch those gorgeous breasts of yours bounce."

"I don't care," I said honestly. "I'm pretty sure you can make me come from any position."

He chuckled, then pulled out, sending another tremor through me. "Damn right."

The bed dipped as he joined me on it, pulling me on top of him. My nipples brushed against his chest, and I moaned as the hair there rubbed my sensitive skin. I pushed myself up enough that I was able to get my hand around his cock and hold him in place. My pussy throbbed with the need to get him inside me again, and I let out a soft sigh as I sank down on him.

"Syll," he groaned, his head falling back and his eyes closing.

I put my hands on his chest, but I didn't close my eyes. I didn't want to miss a moment of this. I'd known he was hot before but seeing him naked...fuck. Every line and muscle defined.

Lickable.

And because I wanted to, I leaned down and ran my tongue around one of his nipples.

"Fuck," he hissed, eyes flying open.

I took his nipple between my teeth and his body arched, driving his cock painfully deep.

"Little minx," he said as he surged upward.

His mouth crashed into mine, teeth bruising my already-swollen lips. I worked my hips back and forth, desperate to find release again. Desperate to bring him with me this time. I dug my nails into his shoulders, fighting through the burn of my thigh muscles.

"Are you going to come again?" he asked as he bit his way down my neck, hard enough that I suspected he'd left marks.

"Mm-hm." I let my head fall back, exposing my throat. "You this time too."

"Maybe," he said.

His teeth sunk into my breast and my entire body jerked.

"Ask me what I need to come, Syll."

"What do you need to come?" I obediently repeated.

"Tell me," he said. "Tell me what you want me to do to you."

I closed my eyes and felt the word before I spoke it. "Everything. I want you to do everything."

He laughed again, a slow, warm caress of sound over my skin. "I'm going to need you to be specific."

"Fuck me. Lick me." I let the words spill from my mouth even as the pleasure reached a near-painful point I'd never felt before. All the things I'd ever wanted to say but had held back in the past, I told him. "I want your mouth on my pussy. Your tongue in my cunt. I want to taste you. Suck your cock. I want you to spank me again."

He pulled me tight against him and put his mouth next to my ear. "Do you want me to fuck your ass?"

I shuddered, so close I could almost taste it.

"Tell me, Syll. Tell me that you want me to fuck your ass."

"I do."

The last word turned into a cry as he flipped me onto my back and slammed into me twice, sending sparks exploding behind my eyes. The second time, he growled my name, and his body tensed above me as he came. He ground down against me, pushing me over the edge one more time before I passed out.

MY FIRST THOUGHT was that I was laying on possibly the most comfortable bed in the history of beds. My second thought was that my bed wasn't even close to this comfortable, which meant I wasn't in my bed.

I rolled over, waiting to feel my hand smack into Billy, to hear him mumble a curse before falling asleep again. When my arm thumped against sheets, my brain began to try to figure out what was wrong.

Billy's bed was more uncomfortable than mine. And his sheets were scratchy. And they generally smelled like week-old sex and sweat. If I wanted clean sheets, I usually had to make the bed myself. Sometimes I thought he had me come to his place whenever he wanted his sheets changed.

These sheets were soft. Expensive.

And they smelled amazing. Freshly laundered, but it was more than that. They smelled like...

Shit.

They didn't smell like shit. They smelled like *Jax*.

My eyes flew open, and I sat up in a rush.

I hadn't drunk enough last night to be hungover, which was good, but I also hadn't drunk enough to not be able to remember what had happened, which was bad.

Because now I remembered *everything*.

His chest under my hands, all those firm muscles, and other firm things that fit inside me as if we'd...

I shook my head. I wasn't going to go down that road. If I started thinking about what had happened, I'd have to think about how I felt about it, and I really didn't want to do that.

Jax wasn't here, so I scrambled out of bed, grabbing my clothes and yanking them on as quickly as I could. My jeans were still damp from the snow, reminding me that we'd gotten a storm last night. I hurried over to the window, sending up a silent prayer that I'd be able to find a cab to take me home.

We'd gotten a good eight inches or so, but we were Bostonians. The roads were cleared, and people were out doing their normal things. I breathed a sigh of relief. I could get out of here without trying to find Jax. And I really didn't want to see him right now. Maybe ever.

Yes, that would be good. Never seeing him again, never having to think about how he'd made me come more times in one night...

Nope. I wasn't going there.

I was going home.

I gave myself a congratulatory pat on the back when I managed to get down to the sidewalk without getting lost in Jax's insanely massive house *and* without seeing him. Then again, for all I knew, he'd left hours ago.

Since I hadn't opened the bar last night, I'd need to have it open tonight, giving me the chance to focus on work and forget everything else. Including the part of yesterday that had been less orgasms and more seeing my boyfriend cheating on me.

As I showered, I started going through a mental list of everything I had to do. I went through every detail twice, trying not to think about how ordering more scotch made me think about how I'd tasted the smooth liquid on Jax's tongue.

By the time I headed to the office, I felt more in control, more like my old self.

No, I decided. I felt *better* than my old self. I didn't have that nagging voice in the back of my head telling me that I needed to call Billy, make time for Billy...basically, a whole bunch of stuff about Billy. And now I didn't have to think about him at all.

And I wasn't. Thinking about him. Or Jax. I was thinking about filling out my order sheet for February.

I was half-way through the list when I thought I heard something. When I glanced out into the bar, however, everything seemed fine, so I went back to my work. I wanted to get this done before we opened. Once Gilly came in, she and I were going to have a hell of a lot to talk about.

I'd mentally prepared a third of my half of the conversation when I heard something else. I got up this time, going out into the bar. I made it a handful of steps before I saw that I wasn't alone.

"Excuse me, we're closed..." My voice trailed off as my brain registered the large man in the black ski mask standing in front of me.

I didn't care how snowy or cold it was. A guy in a ski mask walks into a bar, and it's not the beginning of a joke; it's a robbery.

"You've been given several opportunities to do the right thing, Miss Reeve, but you've failed."

Before I could figure out if someone would even hear me if I screamed, pain exploded across the left side of my face. I hadn't seen him move, and now I couldn't see him at all because my eye was watering as I tried to catch my breath.

A second blow followed the first, knocking me to the ground. I yelled in pain, wrapping my hands around my head to protect it. He drove his foot into my stomach twice, sending shockwaves of pain through my torso, and driving all the air from my lungs.

I coughed and gasped, everything in me focusing on how much I hurt, but I still heard him speak.

"You stay away from Jax Hunter, and the next time Mr. Jones comes to make an offer on this shithole, you do the smart thing and accept it."

TWENTY-ONE

JAX

When I got out of the shower, I thought I was prepared to have an adult conversation with Syll about where things could possibly go from here. Not that I had a clue what I wanted to say. I was just ready for the conversation.

I checked the bathroom, the kitchen, the whole house, thinking that maybe she'd tried to find me and had gotten lost, but she wasn't anywhere. She'd left.

I might've been a guy who'd done the one-night stand thing more than once, but I'd never left without at least telling the woman goodbye. Then again, this hadn't been the most traditional of hook-ups. We'd both been hurting and needed to get our minds off of things. Conversation hadn't really been on my mind.

I was in the middle of making myself a highly-caffeinated beverage when my phone rang. I checked it – just in case Syll had left something here – but it wasn't her. It was Ms. K.

"Hello?"

"Jax, it's Ms. K. I'm sorry to be calling you so soon after..." Her voice cracked.

"It's quite all right," I said softly. "How can I help you?"

"I need you and your brothers to come down to my office to discuss some terms in your grandfather's will. I know they'll want to be returning to their homes after the funeral, so I think it's best for you to come in as soon as possible."

I closed my eyes. The last thing I wanted to do was sit in a room with my brothers and hear my grandfather's will being read, but Ms. K was right. It'd be selfish of me to ask them to hold off because I was having a bad couple of days. I was hardly alone on that count.

Still...

"I'm sure there's a lot of paperwork to be done," I said. "Isn't that something we can do via mail? I mean, I know snail mail isn't really popular nowadays, but contracts are sent through the post office all the time."

There was a moment of silence, and then Ms. K asked, "What do you think you need to sign?"

I took a sip of my coffee before answering. "After our parents died, my brothers and I inherited our father's shares in the company. Technically, Grandfather was still the majority shareholder, but he named me CEO, so I assumed he has some provisions about me maintaining my position. Shifting around his shares and estate to make sure we all get an even inheritance."

"It's a bit more complicated than that," she said after a brief pause. "Look, it wouldn't be fair to tell you and not your brothers. I need to have you all together at the same time."

My gut churned, and it had little to do with what happened with Syll, or even my lack of breakfast. Something wasn't right, and I had a bad feeling whatever it was Ms. K had to tell us, it was going to affect my life more than my brothers.

Wonderful.

"I can be at your office in an hour if you want to call my brothers and ask them to come in too."

After we ended the call, I added a splash of Highland Park to my coffee. I was going to need it.

TWENTY-TWO
SYLL

I didn't like this bed. It wasn't nearly as comfortable as Jax's bed, and the sheets were rough. And sticky with something. And cold. And it was shaking...

No, *I* was shaking. Or, rather, someone was shaking me.

That was weird.

Why was someone shaking me in my bed?

And why did my bed smell funny?

"Syll! Wake up!"

I knew that voice, but it wasn't one that I wanted to hear. I was mad at Billy. I couldn't quite remember why at this moment, but I knew that hearing him say my name made me want to throw up and hit him, or maybe throw up on him *and* hit him.

"Syll! If you don't wake up, I'm going to call 911."

It was the urgency in his voice that finally made me realize that something was seriously wrong.

And then I remembered.

Someone had come into the bar and hurt me.

It was odd, but I hadn't even realized I was in pain until the memories came forward, and then it was like everything hurt all at once. The pain forced my consciousness up through the darkness that I'd been swimming in.

"Fuck," I groaned as I tried to open my eyes. The right one felt gummy, like something was trying to glue my eyelashes together, but I managed to get it open. The left one, however, felt hot and swollen, and no matter how much I tried, I couldn't see a thing out of it.

"Thank God," Billy said. "I was afraid I was going to have to call an ambulance. What happened?"

I pushed myself up, taking note of how my entire arm felt bruised but not broken. That was good, because every breath felt like someone was stabbing me in the lungs, and I had a bad feeling I'd cracked some ribs.

And I didn't even want to see if my face looked as awful as it felt.

When I was eight or nine, we'd had this crazy snowfall that had closed school for an entire week. We'd never been able to take vacations when I was a kid, both because of money and because of not having anyone to cover the bar, but that week, Dad had left one of his friends in charge for a couple days and took me somewhere outside of Boston where there were huge hills covered with snow. We'd taken his old sled down dozens of times, and at the end of the day, I'd begged him for just one more time. He'd given in, and on that pass, we were a bit further to the side than we had been before, and we caught a rock. It sent us into the trees, and I'd hit the trunk of a pine face first.

This felt worse.

"Let's get you up," Billy said as he bent over and wrapped one arm around my waist.

It felt wrong, him touching me, but my head was throbbing, and I couldn't exactly remember why it was wrong. Besides, I wasn't sure I could get to my feet on my own. When I was standing, however, he didn't let me go.

"Babe, you look awful. What happened?"

I leaned against the bar, sucking in a breath at the pressure on my bruised back. He kicked me. The bastard who'd broken into my bar had punched me in the face at least twice. And then he'd kicked me. That was why my ribs hurt.

Dammit.

"The guy who trashed the place came back." My mouth tasted like blood, and while my cheek hurt with the movement, I didn't feel any empty spaces in my gums.

Hooray for me. I got the shit beat out of me, and I still had all my teeth.

"Everything looks fine."

Billy's inane comment had me turning my head to look at him, and now I recalled why I didn't want him touching me.

I managed to take a step to the side, so his arm fell away from me. "Fine? Do I look fine to you?"

"You know what I mean." He scowled at me. "The bar looks fine."

Except the blood on the floor where I'd been laying. That was going to be a bitch to get out of the wood grain. "I need ice."

"You need to go to the hospital," he said. "Come on, babe, let me take you."

"*Babe?*" I echoed as I remembered why I didn't want him near me anymore. "You lost the right to call me that anymore."

"Don't be that way." He reached for me, and I slapped his hand away.

"If you want to do something for me, then get me some ice, but don't touch me."

For a moment, I thought he was going to tell me to fuck myself and walk right back out the door, but after a second, he headed for the kitchen.

Had he come here to talk to me about what happened? He hadn't called or texted, so I didn't think that was it, but then again, he'd probably realized that I wouldn't answer any calls or texts from him. Anyone who knew me would understand that I wouldn't want to see him yet, and definitely not by ambush, but being clueless really wasn't a good enough reason for him to be here.

Especially since I'd told him a few years back that I'd cut off his balls if I caught him cheating on me. Granted, I'd been plastered at the time, but it still seemed like the sort of thing a man wouldn't forget, considering the usual attachment men had to their balls.

"Here."

He shoved a towel full of ice at me, the expression on his face something that would've been at place on a tantrum-throwing preschooler.

I took the ice and held it to my face, hissing at the pain the contact brought with it. I was going to need some heavy-duty painkillers to get through work tonight. Tequila would probably work just as well, but after the unwise choice I'd made last night when inebriated, I was going to lay off the alcohol for a while.

"Thank you," I mumbled, closing my eyes. I let the cold seep into my battered face, numbing those screaming nerves. I would've loved to stand there and enjoy the ice's effects, but I could hear Billy breathing from where he was standing next to me.

"Are you sure you don't need to go to the hospital?"

I sighed. "No." I didn't bother to explain to him that I didn't have the money for a hospital visit. If he'd been paying attention at all, he would've known it.

"Why don't we sit down," he said, "so we can talk without tiring you out."

And any gratitude I was feeling for him finding me and then getting me ice was gone. He hadn't gotten the ice to take care of me. He'd done it because it would get us to what he'd come here for quicker. It was still all about him.

I shuffled over to the closest table and sat down. No use in expending more energy than was absolutely necessary.

"All right, Billy," I said. "Let's have the conversation. Tell me why you're here."

He had the audacity to look hurt. "I'm here because I didn't like the way we left things yesterday. I figured I'd give you some time to cool off, and it was a good thing I came over too. Who knows how long you would've been laying there if I hadn't."

Telling him that I would've eventually woken up on my own would've just prolonged the conversation, so I kept my mouth shut and hoped he'd hurry the fuck up and say what he'd come here to say.

When he realized I wasn't going to thank him again, he frowned, but continued, "We've been together too long to let something like that destroy it all. I mean, it's not like you were innocent in all of it. You said yourself you'd come over to tell me you'd cheated on me."

I held up a hand. "I made out with someone else, yes, but I stopped it, and came to see you to make things right. I wasn't fucking other people for months and only admitted to it when it was too late to deny it."

He rubbed the back of his head. "I'm sorry, Syll, all right? Is that what you want to hear? That I'm sorry?"

I would've wanted to hear it if I thought for a moment he meant it. It'd be easy to accept the apology and go back to the comfortable patterns of our relationship. I could pretend like I believed he regretted what he'd done, and not just that he'd gotten caught.

But what he said after I caught him, that was stuck in my head. It had been cruel and mean-spirited. *That* was how he really felt – who he really was – and I refused to allow him to treat me that way.

"I don't want you to say anything you don't mean," I said. "And I know you don't mean any of what you just said."

"This is bullshit, Syll. You can't tell me you're seriously going to throw away the years we've had together over this?"

The fact that he was reacting in anger, throwing this on me instead of taking responsibility for his behavior, and telling me that he'd do whatever it took to make things right – like I'd been prepared to do last night – just convinced me that I was making the right choice.

"I think you threw us out way before I caught you with Ariene." I took the ice off my face to see him better, and then remembered that I couldn't see out of that eye anyway. "Or are you going to sit there and lie to my face and say that yesterday was the first time you've ever cheated on me?"

Color flooded his face, and he clenched his hands into fists. "That...that's...Syll...that's not..."

I held up my hand. "Don't bother. I'm not going to believe you."

"Don't you even want to know why?"

A chill that had nothing to do with ice crept into my blood. "You made that perfectly clear last night."

The bar door opened, and I jerked around, ignoring the pain as adrenaline flooded me, flight or fight making my heart hammer against my aching ribs. It wasn't the masked man though.

It was Ariene, strolling in here like yesterday had never happened.

I pushed myself to my feet. "Get out."

She stopped half-way across the floor, her eyes widening as she took in my face.

"I want both of you out of my bar." I looked over at Billy as he stood. "Now."

She crossed her arms over her chest. "But, I have a shift tonight."

I stared at her. "You don't give a shit about your shifts. You hate it here, and always make sure I know it. So, I'm going to give you a gift. You're fired."

Her pretty face twisted into an ugly mask. "You can't fire

me. I haven't done shit wrong."

I wanted to tell her that I damn well had a reason to fire her, but then I realized she was right. People liked to think that because a person owned a business, they could hire and fire on a whim, but that wasn't true. Or, rather, they could try it, but if the former employee decided to sue, they'd probably have a case for wrongful termination. And even though Ariene had constantly complained about her job, she hadn't been late or left early. She hadn't taken extra breaks. And while she had been fucking my boyfriend, she hadn't done it at work.

All of which meant I couldn't fire her without her using her relationship with Billy as a reason to sue me.

But that didn't mean I had to put up with having her around today.

"Okay. I can't fire you, but that doesn't mean I can't change your schedule. We haven't been getting a lot of customers the last few nights, so I think Gilly and I can handle it."

Ariene glared at me. "You can't send me home and let Gilly stay."

I lifted my chin. "I can. She has seniority."

"Bitch," she muttered.

I let that one go, because I wanted them out. "Also, a word to the wise, if things don't pick up, I may need to cut your hours. Again, Gilly has seniority, so her hours get priority. You might want to start looking for another job."

Ariene took a step toward me, but Billy stepped between us. "Let's go, babe. We don't need this."

He looked over his shoulder at me, and I made a little shooing motion with my hand. The quicker they got out, the quicker I could clean up. I waited until they closed the door behind them, then crossed to the door and locked it.

I locked the door between the bar and my apartment too, then after a minute, moved a chair in front of it. I wasn't going to get caught off-guard again.

TWENTY-THREE
JAX

We sat in a half-circle in front of Ms. K's desk, all of us trying not to look at each other. My brothers' motives were probably like my own. We'd all loved Grandfather in our own way, and we'd all mourn in our own way. None of us had ever shared our grief, not when it'd been Grandma Olive, not even when it had been our parents and Aimee. We were just too different, and it hurt too much.

"Thank you for coming so quickly. I know this has been hard on all of you." Ms. K's own eyes were red-rimmed, but she sounded professional and collected. I'd always liked and respected her, but my estimation of her had grown immensely over the past few days. "Your grandfather had hoped that he'd be able to rewrite his will back to what it had been, but..."

"*Back?*" I echoed.

"Originally, your grandfather had intended to split his shares of the company between the four of you. The same with the estate. He had provisions in place in case you wanted to change some things around. Buy out each other's shares, or various parts of the estate."

That made sense. I doubted my brothers would want the

house, and they might not even want their shares in the company. At least I knew they wouldn't have a problem with me running things. None of them had said a word when Grandfather had appointed me the CEO. I'd been the only one who'd even wanted to work there in the first place. They all had different interests. Business was the only thing I'd ever wanted to do. The only thing I'd ever been good at.

"He always knew us well enough to know we liked different things," I said.

One of my brothers made a sound like a smothered laugh, but I didn't look to see who it was. Ms. K, however, glared to my right, so I assumed it had been Blake.

"He did," she said. "And he loved the four of you very much."

"Ms. K, you said this was an urgent matter," Cai spoke up. "I don't think offering up platitudes requires urgency."

Leave it to Cai to say it flat-out like that. He'd never had any tact. Grandfather had always said it was a good thing Cai had gone into a medical field that didn't require subtlety. He would've been shit at doing what I did. Business dealings like mine required both strength and diplomacy.

Ms. K gave him a sharp look. "Is saying how much your grandfather loved you a platitude?"

"No," Cai agreed. "But that's personal, and this is business."

She flinched, and I was tempted to turn around and smack my kid brother upside the back of his head like I had when we were kids, and he'd said something stupid. Couldn't he see how upset she was? Hadn't they realized that her relationship with Grandfather had been more than professional?

"I think what my brother's trying to say is that we'd like to hear what you needed to talk to us about so that we won't have it weighing on our minds during the funeral." Slade cut into the conversation with his usual mellow tone.

He did that a lot. Inserted himself into situations that were tense and either said something funny, or like now, something that gave a simple explanation and diffused the tension.

"I don't see why everyone's being so damn polite," Blake muttered under his breath. "None of us are any other time."

Ms. K shuffled a couple papers on the desk, her cheeks pink.

"Let's just get this over with, okay?" I said. "I'm sure you'd like to be alone."

Her eyes met mine briefly, and I saw her gratitude in them. I wondered again how little I must've been paying attention if I hadn't known about her relationship with Grandfather.

"As I was saying." Her voice was stronger than it had been. "He'd hoped to have the will changed back, but because he hadn't, it stands as is."

"What does that mean?" Cai asked.

"Did he write us all out?" Blake slid his eyes toward me. "Or everyone but Jax?"

"He didn't write any of you out," Ms. K said. She seemed to have regained her composure and handled the interruptions easily. "It's not the division of the estate that's changed, but rather the stipulations that come along with it."

"Stipulations?" Blake snorted a laugh. "Figures the old man would set up rules we have to follow to get an inheritance we would've gotten from our dad anyway."

And the tension was back.

"He can keep it," Blake continued. "I don't need his money."

I turned as I heard him move, catching him in the middle of standing up.

"Sit down, Blake." I didn't shout, but I used the same tone on him that I'd used when he was a kid. To my surprise, he stopped, glared at me, and then sat back down. "Let's hear her out."

"Whatever," he muttered, crossing his arms.

After a beat, Ms. K continued with her explanation.

"Your grandfather didn't make a list of rules for you to follow." She almost sounded scandalized by the idea. "He wasn't like that."

I could think of plenty of times in my life he'd been exactly like that, and I knew my brothers could too. I didn't say anything though, and they'd apparently either learned their lesson about interrupting or decided it wasn't worth the time it would take.

"What he wanted was for you to resolve your differences."

I waited for the punch line because there had to be one. There was no way that our grandfather would've made *that* a condition.

"What's that supposed to mean?" I finally asked.

"It means that he was aware that the four of you had problems with each other, and he didn't want you to go through the rest of your lives staying mad at each other." She paused, and then added, "Everything will be held in trust until such time as I can say that you're reconciled."

"What, exactly, does that mean?" I asked slowly. "For the business."

"It means that, until your grandfather's shares are distributed, no one really has majority shares in the company since the four of you have an equal number of shares."

"That could seriously fuck up the business." I leaned forward, forcing my voice to stay low. "I can't see Grandfather doing that. Hunter Enterprises is everything – *was* everything – to him."

"He made a provision," she said, "that if you were working on reconciliation, there's a temporary grant of ownership that will allow you to still oversee the day-to-day workings of the company."

Okay, that was something.

She stood. "I'm going to step out for a few minutes, let you talk."

She didn't say anything else as she left us alone, silence

filling the room. I didn't look at them, but I knew they were doing the same thing I was doing. Waiting for someone else to say something.

"I don't know what she's talking about," I finally said. "Just because we're brothers doesn't mean we have to be best friends. We just drifted apart. Siblings do it all the time."

"You would think that," Blake muttered.

I turned to look at him. "What's that supposed to mean?"

"Don't worry about it," he said, his expression mutinous as he got up. "I don't expect you to get it."

The three of us watched as he stormed out, looking, even at twenty-eight, like the little boy who used to get so angry when told it was time for bed. I looked at Slade and then at Cai, wondering if either one of them thought this was necessary.

"I need to call in," Cai said. "I said I would as soon as I knew more about the arrangements."

As he walked out, he was reciting a list under his breath, something that consisted of lots of scientific words I didn't understand.

Slade gave me a smile that didn't quite reach his eyes. "What do you say we figure out what it is we have to say to each other to get this taken care of? Then we can go back to our regular lives and never have to think about each other except to mail Christmas cards." He stood. "It seems pretty clear that's what everyone wants."

As he left, I wondered about what he said. Was that what he thought?

Was it what *I* thought?

Was it what I wanted?

And, more importantly, did it even matter anymore?

TWENTY-FOUR
SYLL

It was a slow Tuesday night, but that was good. It meant that I didn't have to feel guilty about telling Ariene not to come in. Gilly was able to handle things without any problems, and it made for a more peaceful work environment. I hadn't told her about what happened yet, but she was smart. Plus, she'd already suspected what Billy had been up to with Ariene. I had a feeling that if she saw me with Ariene, she'd figure it out. I planned on telling her later tonight when she'd have to decide between going home at a fairly decent hour and going over to Ariene's and bitch-slapping her, then going to Billy's and bitch-slapping *him*.

Right now, however, I was busy training Doug. Doug was my new bartender. He'd never done it before, but he assured me he'd drunk at least half of the drinks we served. He looked and sounded like the stereotype of a frat boy. Which basically meant he was good-looking and not-too-bright but loved to have fun.

I just hoped he could do more than smile at me and nod. For the last fifteen minutes, that's all he'd been doing.

It was better than what everyone else was doing when they saw me though. I'd put on more makeup than I'd ever worn before, doing my best to hide what that guy had done to me, but my left eye was still swollen almost completely shut, and no amount of foundation could fix that. Only a few customers had asked about it, but they'd seemed to accept my story about how I'd taken a tumble down the stairs.

Gilly would see right through that though. The bar was just one story.

Which was why I'd been keeping my distance, using training Doug as an excuse. But now we were closing in on the end of what I could reasonably call training. I'd gone through all the nit-picking stuff, and he'd watched me make drinks for the past three hours. Now, it was time for him to start mixing. I'd keep watching him, but things were slow enough that Gilly would want to talk to me. I just had to decide what I wanted to tell her.

"All right, time's up." Gilly's voice came from behind me.

"What do you mean?" I asked without turning around.

"I've given you space because you clearly don't want to talk about whatever's got you moving around like that."

I closed my eyes. Shit. I should've known she would've already figured out that something was up.

"You need to talk to me, Syll."

I took a slow breath, but not a deep one because my ribs still hurt like hell, and then I turned around.

Gilly let loose with a string of curses that had half the bar staring at her. She came around the bar, ignoring the looks she was getting. "What the fuck happened?"

What the hell. Might as well give the excuse a try. "I fell."

Her eyes narrowed down to slits. "Don't bullshit me, Syll. If Billy did this to you, I'll cut his fucking balls off and stuff them down his throat."

"It wasn't Billy," I said. "Someone broke into the bar and beat me up."

"Like hell. You think I didn't notice who's not here right

now? Ariene. And now that I see you, and no Billy anywhere in sight, I think the shit hit the fan."

I sighed and pressed my fingers to my temples. "I told Ariene she didn't need to be here."

Gilly leaned one hip against the bar and folded her arms. "If you'd said that without gritting your teeth, I might've believed you. Now, spill."

"I'm telling the truth about this." I gestured to my face. "The guy came in, beat me up and threatened me. He told me to...make wise choices." I decided that leaving out the part about Jax wasn't lying. It wasn't relevant. "Billy didn't hurt me. In fact, he found me after it happened."

"Why the hell aren't you at the hospital? They couldn't have let you go so soon, not when the police are involved...fuck. You didn't call the cops, did you?"

I shook my head, swallowing a wince at the pain. "I can't afford to lose any more business. If I called them, they'd consider the bar a crime scene again, and I'd lose even more business."

A different sort of concern crossed her face. "What aren't you telling me?"

"A lot," I admitted. "Some because I didn't want you to worry, but some because I didn't want to hear you say *I told you so.*"

"What would I – that fucking piece of shit!" She straightened. "That *fucking bastard!*"

"Keep your voice down," I warned. "This isn't something I want the whole world to hear, okay?"

She kept going with the insults, but at least she lowered her voice.

"You were right. He was cheating on me with Ariene, and it's been going on for months. And I don't think it's the first time he's done it."

She reached out to touch my left arm, then glanced at my face, and switched to the right arm. She squeezed my shoulder.

"I'm sorry. I wish I hadn't been right."

"I know." I met my friend's gaze. "I went over to his place yesterday, and Ariene opened the door. Words were exchanged. He came by today to try to get me back, and that's when he found me."

"How do you know this wasn't him setting you up? Like so he could come in and play the hero?"

I laughed. "I know it wasn't him, because he wasn't a hero. In fact, all he cared about was getting me to a place where he could say what he wanted to say."

"Fucker."

I shrugged. "Fortunately, he's not my problem anymore."

"But you still have one." She lifted a brow, studying me closely. "Don't you?"

I nodded. "Someone's trying to buy my bar, and they're not being subtle about it."

"I don't understand."

"I've gotten a couple offers to buy the bar, and I turned them both down. Someone connected to at least one of them trashed the bar and left a threatening note. Then one of the guys showed up at the cemetery on Sunday." I didn't have to tell her what Sunday had been. She knew. She'd been with me on the actual day, and on the first anniversary.

"I ever see the asshole who did that, I'm going to knock out his teeth."

I didn't doubt it. "The man who hurt me, he's connected too."

Gilly sighed. "Syll, what am I going to do with you?"

That was an excellent question, but one I couldn't answer because someone had just come into the bar and he required all my attention.

"Who is *that* tall drink of water?" Gilly asked. "I'd like to ride him like a Mustang."

I gave her a sideways look, but there wasn't any jealousy in it. Jax wasn't Gilly's type.

"Hey, can I get some scotch? Best you've got."

I blinked at the abrupt request. Not even a hello. I hadn't been expecting declarations of love and commitment, but he wasn't even looking at me. He was staring at his phone just like every other jackass douchebag who thought the world revolved around them.

"You would not believe the day I've had."

"I've got this," I said to Doug and Gilly. My friend gave me a strange look, but I motioned for her to go. Doug ambled down to the other side of the bar to take a couple orders there.

I poured two fingers of my best scotch and set the glass in front of Jax.

He drained it all in one swallow without looking up from his phone. "I got a call from my grandfather's attorney, wanting my brothers and me to come into her office. Get this, he put conditions in his will, things that my brothers and I must do before we receive our inheritance. It's not about the money, you know. It's him trying to control–"

"Jax–"

He kept going like I hadn't said a word. "Like we aren't all adults with our own lives. He just expected us to drop everything because he snapped his fingers with no regard for anything we might–"

I'd had enough.

"Look, I'm sorry you've had a bad day, but you're not the only one," I snapped. "My day hasn't exactly been sunshine and roses."

He finally raised his head, and I watched the annoyance in his eyes turn into shock, then concern, then anger.

"What hap–"

I cut him off. "I get that you're upset about your grandfather, and that sucks, but you have three brothers. Some people don't have any family." Everything that I'd been trying to hold in came spilling out. "Some of us have to fight and scrape to hold on to every little bit we have, and we have to do it all alone because there's hardly anyone we can trust. We don't all have money to buy whatever whim we're currently jonesing for, only to throw it away as soon as we get bored with it."

He frowned at me, reaching across the bar to touch my hand. "That's not what I did. I mean, that's not what last night—"

"I don't want to talk about last night," I interrupted. "That's not what this is about. It's about you coming in here, plopping your ass down at the bar, and acting like you're the only person here who's had a shitty day."

I knew I was being a bit of a bitch. His grandfather had just died, and I knew how much that hurt him. I'd seen him at the hospital. Just because he was going on about his brothers and the will didn't mean he was *upset* about either of those things. Sometimes, when people were upset, they latched on to unrelated things.

Like me going off about his complaints because I was having some issues of my own.

"I need some air," I announced, turning away from him.

He was around the bar and in my personal space before I'd gone more than a few steps. Damn, he smelled good.

"Is there somewhere we can talk alone?"

I nodded. "You remember the way?"

The heat in his gaze made me blush.

"I remember *all* of it."

And so did I.

Fuck me. I had a bad feeling this wasn't going to go my way.

TWENTY-FIVE
JAX

What the *fuck* had happened to Syll?!

I couldn't believe I hadn't noticed when I'd first come into the bar. I'd been thinking about everything that'd happened to me today, and how I wanted a drink and to talk to someone. Syll had been the first person to come to mind, which made sense since I didn't really have much in the way of friends. I'd been almost to the bar when I realized just how real that statement was. On the extremely rare occasions in the past I'd needed to talk to someone, I'd gone to my grandfather. But I couldn't go to him anymore.

I wished I could blame my lack of attention to a new bout of grief, but that wasn't it. I'd simply been so focused on myself that I'd never considered anything else. Or any*one* else.

She deserved better.

I'd known that from the moment I met her.

And I'd still wanted her last night.

Fuck the past tense. I wanted her now. One time with her wasn't enough.

But this wasn't about me anymore. The moment I'd looked up and seen the bruises she tried to hide, the swollen left side of her face, everything became about her. Even when she was ranting, I could only think about how to take care of her.

I took her hand, not because she needed me to lead her, but because I needed to touch her, and until I knew more, I didn't want to accidentally touch her somewhere that would cause her pain.

As we headed toward the back, I allowed myself a moment to appreciate the irony at the desire to not cause pain. I wasn't a true sadist, and I wasn't the sort of sadist who enjoyed anything non-consensual or intentionally harmful. In fact, the thought of causing Syll any sort of pain that wouldn't result in her extreme pleasure went against every fiber of my being.

If I found out that an actual person was responsible for how banged up she looked, they would have an easier time turning themselves into the police and facing assault charges than what would happen if I got my hands on them.

She tugged me to a stop before we reached the door to her apartment. Her office was fairly quiet, and it was empty, but a part of me was disappointed that she didn't want me in her place again.

Then again, that hadn't exactly ended well, so I supposed being in a neutral place was best for the talk we needed to have.

"All right," she said as she tugged her hand out of mine. "We're alone. What did you want to talk about?"

"Are you kidding me?" I gestured toward her face. "What the hell happened to you?"

She sighed with the weariness of someone who'd told the same story so many times that it was almost painful to say it one more time.

"I fell down the stairs."

"What stairs?" I wasn't going to let her get away with some bullshit story. "There aren't any stairs in this building."

"How do you know?"

I almost growled at her. "Because I've seen the blueprints. Before I came here the first time, I looked over the building information available to the public. This is one-story, with no basement." I took a step toward her and softened my voice. "Talk to me."

She folded her arms across her chest and looked away. "Someone broke in earlier today and did this."

My temper, usually kept under lock and key, flared. "You aren't covering for that asshole ex of yours, are you?"

She shook her head, a small smile touching her lips. "Gilly basically asked me the same thing. He's still an asshole, but he didn't do this. The guy wore a ski mask, but I would've recognized Billy's voice. Besides, he was way too tall to be Billy. I think it was the same guy who trashed the place."

"What did the cops say?"

She looked down at her hands. "I didn't call them."

"Dammit, Syll, you need to report this!"

Her head lifted so I could see the sparks in her eyes. "And you need to mind your own damn business. This is *my* bar, *my* life. I'll take care of things the same way I have since my dad died. *Myself*. You might not be used to a woman who prefers to do things herself rather than relying on a man, but I was raised to be indep–"

I cut off the rest of what she was going to say by covering her mouth with mine. I kissed her carefully, not wanting to aggravate her injuries, but I wanted nothing more than to plunder those sweet, dark depths with my tongue until she was soft and pliant in my arms.

I should have known better.

The moment I lifted my head, her hand went up to slap me. I automatically caught her wrist, and her eyes went wide. The flash of fear I saw in them cut me, and I promised myself that I would do whatever I could to make sure she knew she was safe with me. No matter what had happened between us in the past, or what would happen in the future, she needed to know that I'd never give her reason to be afraid of me.

I brought her hand to my mouth and kissed the palm. I didn't release her hand but rather began to massage it as I spoke, "I'm sorry. After last night, I thought it would be okay for me to surprise you with a kiss. I shouldn't have assumed."

"I...thank you." Uncertainty clouded her features. "I shouldn't have tried to slap you. This time." Her shoulders slumped. "I'm just having a really shitty day."

I gave her a small smile. "Me, too."

I didn't tell her that my bad day started when I realized she'd left without a word. This wasn't about blame or guilt. It was about something entirely different. We weren't in a club, and we'd never discussed anything along the lines of a Dom / sub relationship, but the Dom in me was determined to protect and care for her.

I cupped her chin, tipping her face back until she was looking at me. "How can I help you? Just tell me."

"I don't want to talk," she said. "And I don't want to think."

"I think I can manage that." I gave her one of my most charming grins, and for the first time in a long time, I meant it.

"I'm not expecting anything from you," she continued. "And I'm not offering anything."

"I thought you said you didn't want to think or talk anymore."

She gave me a hard, searching look, and then nodded. "You're right. I don't."

This time, she kissed me.

I let her take charge of it, and my Dominant side didn't even argue. With everything that had happened to her recently being so far beyond her control, I knew she needed to feel at least some semblance of it somewhere. When the hands that had gripped my shirt softened against me, I took over.

I ran my hands down her back, paying close attention to any

sign of discomfort so I could shift my caress. It was one thing to tease after a punishment, and something else to play off a true injury. I palmed her ass and lifted her onto the desk. A few papers fell to the floor, but I ignored them as I started to unbutton her shirt.

Once I had it undone, I broke the kiss and let my gaze fall to her bra. It was nothing fancy, probably the easiest one to put on with her injuries, but that didn't matter. It was a front clasp.

Hell. Yes.

I flicked it open, mumbling a curse as I lowered my head. She gasped as my tongue circled one nipple, and then the other. They pebbled as the cool air came in to contact with the sensitive skin. I could've spent hours just doing this, but we didn't have hours. Sooner, rather than later, someone was going to realize that she wasn't in the bar, and they'd come looking for her. My money was on the blonde she'd called Gilly.

I needed to make sure we both got off before that happened. Which meant I needed to get her out of her pants.

"Damn jeans," I growled. "Lift up."

She obeyed, and I tugged off her jeans, taking her panties too. They were plain cotton, but I tucked them into my pants pocket anyway. When I raised my eyes, she was watching me with a questioning look on her face.

"You can get them next time." I pushed her knees apart, loving the way she flushed as she opened to my perusal. "Another note for next time: you're going to touch yourself while I watch."

"Why not now?" she asked.

"Because I need to taste your pussy." I sank to my knees. "Now, be a good girl and come whenever you like, but you might want to keep it down if you don't want everyone in the bar to know what I'm doing."

As I lowered my head, she opened her mouth to say something, but all that came out was a low keen. Damn, she tasted amazing. Fresh and clean, reminding me of spring. I licked her again and earned another of those dick-hardening sounds. I needed more time to properly go down on her, tease her until she was panting and begging, taking her so high that she'd see stars. But I didn't have that kind of time now, which meant I was going to have to go with getting her off as quickly as possible.

Her hands came down on my head, fingers digging into my hair, nails scratching my scalp. I gripped her hips as firmly as I dared, holding her in place against my mouth even as she tightened her hold on my head. She didn't need to worry. I wasn't planning on going anywhere until she exploded on my tongue.

I danced around her entrance, sneaking quick dips inside to sample her arousal, and then moved up to her clit. I flicked my tongue against it, and she said my name. Then I pressed the flat of my tongue to it and rubbed the swelling bundle of nerves. That earned a curse and a jolt of pain as she pulled my hair.

I looked up at her as I repeated the combination. Her breasts heaved with every breath, her chest flushed, and nipples hardened. Her head was tilted back, exposing her neck, and I had a momentary image of what it would be like to mark her skin with my teeth, to wrap my fingers around her throat. Not to choke her, but to see just how much she trusted me.

More things to add to my list.

At this rate, we'd be together until next Christmas. The thought didn't disturb me as much as it might once have.

"Jax," she whimpered. "I'm so close. Make me come, please."

I pulled back just far enough to speak. "Have you ever come from oral sex?" Her eyes opened, and she looked down at me. "Tell me, Syll." I made it an order.

She shook her head. "Bil–*he* never liked going down on me, and he didn't like me to tell him..." She paused, then continued, "I don't want to talk about him. The answer's just *no*."

I turned my head and kissed her inner thigh. "Then it'll be my pleasure to give you your first."

I put my mouth on her again, working my tongue over all her sensitive areas, scraping my teeth lightly across her clit, sucking on it, overloading her on sensations until she finally exploded with a desperate cry. She clapped a hand over her mouth as the orgasm ripped through her, muffling the sound, but that was okay for now. One day, I'd want to learn just how loud I could make her scream.

I stood, watching her body twitch and tremble as the pleasure faded.

We weren't done yet.

TWENTY-SIX
SYLL

Wow.

Just...wow.

The couple times I'd managed to convince Billy to go down on me, he'd done it for a couple minutes, then it'd been my turn to reciprocate. Even though I'd never had good oral sex – until a few seconds ago – I'd been able to tell that Billy's attempts had been half-hearted at best. I'd given up even asking after a while, resigning myself to not having that as part of my sex life.

What Jax had just done was better than pretty much every other sexual experience I'd ever had.

I opened my eyes to tell Jax just that, but the words couldn't find their way out of my befuddled brain, especially when I saw him rolling a condom on over his thick shaft. I'd never understood women who described penises as *beautiful*, but when it came to Jax Hunter...

He was a fine specimen of male flesh all the way around.

"Syll." His voice was rough, his eyes dark. "I need to know you want this."

I wasn't even close to considering saying no. Not with him standing there looking all gorgeous, and me sitting on the desk, my legs splayed open, my pussy throbbing with the need to be filled. The need to connect.

Still, I couldn't bring myself to speak above a whisper. "I want you."

He stepped closer, sliding his hands up my legs from knee to thigh, then curling his fingers around my hips. "Put your hands behind your back."

I did as he said, threading my fingers between each other.

"Don't come," he warned. "Not until I tell you to."

I raised an eyebrow. "And what if I do?"

He grinned a dangerous sort of grin. "I can think of all kinds of ways to punish you."

That comment should have made me uneasy, but all I felt was a thrill run down my spine. I could feel the power in his body, the strength there, but he held it back. He knew he didn't have to show off for me to know how strong he was. Unlike Billy, who'd always used every opportunity possible to make people see him as bigger and better.

Then he was pushing inside of me, and all the thoughts in my head flew away. Everything in my brain was reduced to *yes, yes, fuck, yes.*

"Next time," he said as he slid another inch forward, "we're going to play a bit more."

"Play?" The word came out as a squeak.

"Yes, play." He groaned as he sank the rest of the way into me.

He rotated his hips, and I moaned, reaching out to grab his shirt. "You're wearing too many clothes. I want to touch you."

"You are touching me." He sounded amused, but the heat in his eyes was anything but amusing.

"No, I want I want I want..." I let out a cry as he snapped his hips forward. "Fuck yes that. More of that."

He began to move in fast, deep strokes that rubbed against all the right parts of me. "Keep talking."

"What?" I clung to his shoulders, all my attention focused on the point where our bodies connected.

"Keep talking. Tell me what you want."

"Skin." It took an insane effort to manage to get just that word out.

He grabbed the back of his shirt and pulled it over his head without missing a beat. "Better?"

I nodded. I slid my hands down from his shoulders to his chest. Every inch of him was solid as a rock.

He wrapped his arm around my waist, holding me in place as he began to move faster, each new stroke driving the air from my lungs and sending ripples of pleasure across my nerves. I curled forward, every cell in my body vibrating as I struggled to keep myself from coming. I dug my nails into his chest, barely aware of what I was doing.

A bolt of lightning hit me as Jax's thumb pressed against my clit, rubbed it, and I was helpless to do anything but chase the electricity right over the edge. I pressed my face against his chest, used his body to muffle all the sounds I couldn't stop myself from making.

Each new thrust sent me a little higher, and then he buried himself deep once, twice, and came. For a few glorious seconds, we hovered there together, riding the bliss we'd found in each other's bodies.

I didn't want to like him, but I knew I wasn't sitting here, my arms wrapped around him, his forehead resting against mine, just because the sex was good. The scent of sex and whatever spicy soap he used surrounded me. I could feel him, still inside me, and I knew we'd both need to move soon, but in this moment, I was content. Not only content but safe. He wouldn't let anyone hurt me...

I shouldn't be thinking like that.

He wasn't my boyfriend. This was sex, and nothing more. I didn't have to like him to fuck him, so I wasn't going to like him. I'd tolerate him when he wasn't giving me toe-curling orgasms.

And as soon as my brain was functioning enough to communicate effectively, I'd tell him that.

"You didn't keep your hands behind your back," he said as he straightened.

I shivered as he pulled out, the loss of his body heat affecting me as much as the sudden emptiness inside me. He tossed the condom into the trashcan next to the desk and tucked himself back into his pants. Then he bent over, picking up both his shirt and my pants.

"You came without permission."

I sucked in a breath as I slid off the desk, a whole new set of aches joining the others. Despite that, I didn't regret what we'd done. As I eased into my pants, however, I saw some of the papers that had fallen off the desk, and my father's name was still at the top of a couple of them. This was his office, and I'd had sex in here with Billy, and now with a virtual stranger. I couldn't think of a worse way to disrespect Dad's memory than what I'd just done.

"That's two things I need to punish you for."

I looked up as I fixed my shirt, momentarily confused by what he'd said. Then I remembered, and my treacherous body clenched with nearly painful need.

"I need to get back to work," I said, turning away from him.

For a moment, I thought he would grab my arm, turn me around so he could tell me exactly how he was going to punish me. Except he didn't do any of those things.

"Have you ever thought about expanding the bar?"

I turned on my own and saw a thoughtful expression on Jax's face. "Expanding? Did you see how empty it is out there?"

"If you opened all this into one big, open space, it could be more than a bar."

I froze. More than a bar? Was he really making a business pitch *now*?

"I already checked the blueprints to make sure it'd be possible to tear out these walls."

"Are you fucking kidding me?" I shook my head, feeling a bitter laugh wanting to force itself from between my lips. How could I have been so stupid?

"What?" He sounded surprised, but for all I knew, he was that good of an actor.

"Do you still want my bar?" I waited a few moments for an answer, but when it didn't come, I took that as a good enough response. "Get out, and don't come back."

TWENTY-SEVEN

JAX

THE ROOM WAS PACKED, BUT THAT DIDN'T SURPRISE ME. Grandfather had been well-known and well-liked. Well, maybe more like well-respected rather than well-liked. He'd never been the sort of man people talked about liking, but people did always want him around, and it looked like everyone had come out of the woodwork to pay their respects.

"Jax, I haven't seen you in a dog's age."

The old man extending a hand to me looked vaguely familiar, but I couldn't quite place him. I wasn't about to let him know that though. I owed it to Grandfather to maintain the family name, especially since I was going to be the face of the company now.

"Thanks for coming," I said. "Grandfather would have appreciated it."

"He was a great man," he said as he shook my hand enthusiastically. "He'll be missed."

I thanked him and then turned to the next person in line, listening to the same platitudes, the same compliments. I recognized maybe two out of ten, and all of them were from the business world. We were an hour into the calling hours we were holding before the afternoon's service, and I hadn't seen anyone I would've considered a friend. The only family I had left was standing in the receiving line next to me.

We'd ended up standing in birth order completely by chance, which meant I was standing next to Cai, and I supposed that was a good thing since it meant that people didn't get two reticent Hunter brothers in a row since I was used to talking to people I didn't know. Slade would hold his own, and Blake was behaving himself. Ms. K had refused to stand with us, saying it wasn't her place. I hadn't wanted to press the issue, knowing it would only embarrass her to have that personal side of their relationship brought out.

So, she was standing off to one side, out of the way, and trying not to look like she'd been crying. I'd already put a reminder in my phone to send her a huge *thank you* gift tomorrow. She'd said that she couldn't take credit for the service because Grandfather had planned for everything except the date, and that hadn't taken any skill on her part, but I knew she'd put her heart into this. It was everything Grandfather would have wanted.

"Do you actually know any of these people?" Cai asked quietly.

"Some of them," I admitted.

"If you don't know them, why the hell are they here?"

I glared at Blake as his voice carried. "Because it's not all about us."

"Right." He shrugged. "Why should it be about us? We're only the grandsons he raised after our parents died. Why should that make us any more special than someone he met once at a business conference?"

I stepped behind Cai to put me closer to our youngest brother. "This isn't the time or place, Blake. Pull yourself together."

"Let me guess," he sneered, "'we have a reputation to uphold.'"

The muscle popped in my jaw. "The family name might not mean much to you, but it does to me. And I don't have the luxury of running off to another life when this is all over. I live here, I work here. Maybe you could at least try to not act like a total asshole."

"Me?" Blake snapped. "I'm not the one who's been bitching all morning about every little thing."

"I think this is the sort of conversation we could have later," Slade said. "Perhaps when we're not supposed to be grieving for our dead grandfather."

Slade's words had the sobering effect he most likely intended, and we returned to our places in line, polite plastic smiles in place.

Everything began to blur as one hour turned into two, and then we were sitting in strangely comfortable chairs as people took turns talking about what a great man Grandfather was, and how he'd made a difference in so many people's lives. Then it was my turn, and I read a passage Grandfather had pre-selected, and then gave a short speech that he would've approved of. Personal, but unsentimental.

Then, suddenly, it was all over, and the only thing left to do was put Grandfather's ashes in the family crypt. Grandfather had instructed that only us four attend the interment, and as soon as we reached the cemetery, I knew I wasn't the only one who breathed a sigh of relief that we were alone.

"I'm glad that's over," Slade said as he squinted up at the sun. "It was getting tense in there."

"So, what are we going to do about those asinine restrictions to Grandfather's will?" Blake asked. "You think Ms. K will notice if we pretend to play nice?"

"We're brothers." I lifted a shoulder. "There's nothing

wrong with how we act with each other. It's okay that we aren't best friends. Like I said before, not all siblings are."

"Do you really think that our relationships are fine?" Slade rolled his eyes. "Come on, you and Blake nearly came to blows at our grandfather's funeral."

"Because he was being an ass," I said. "He's always an ass. Why is that my fault? Why do I get fucked over because he can't act like a fucking human being at a fucking funeral?"

"Whoa." Blake held up his hands. "What crawled up your ass?"

"In case you hadn't noticed, our grandfather is dead, and some stupid stipulations he set up might put me out of a job and our family's legacy in the hands of some outsider."

Slade shook his head. "No, that's not it. Something's up with you."

I sighed and pinched the bridge of my nose. "Nothing's up with me. I just have a lot going on."

"And does that particular 'a lot' have a name?" Slade asked with that obnoxious grin of his.

"I can't believe you're asking me that here, now." I shook my head.

"I think Grandfather would approve," Slade said. "He's the one who wanted us to reconcile our differences. I think a good place to start would be for you to tell us why you're acting like this."

"Sure, I'm having a problem with this woman, okay? It's nothing important. She's nothing important." I ground my teeth together as I thought about how she kicked me out of her bar a few nights ago after accusing me of just being after the property. "Someone I met when I was scoping out this property. Grandfather had heard that the prices in the area were going up, and I decided this bar would be the perfect place to start a club. I went there to make an offer, and this woman, Syll, she tells me she's not interested. She drives me nuts."

"You're acting like this because of a girl?" Blake started laughing. "That was the last thing I expected to hear."

I shook my head. "I don't want to think about her. In fact, I'll talk about anything *except* Syll."

"All right," Slade said. "Why don't you tell us why you want to start a club? Hunter Enterprises isn't exactly in the business-building business. And definitely not building a dance club."

"I didn't say it was a dance club."

"What kind of club then?" Slade asked, then his brows drew together as he considered the options. "Like some sort of gentlemen's club?"

I considered my brothers for a moment, and then decided I might as well tell them. Maybe it'd get us to some place where we could convince Ms. K that we were doing what Grandfather wanted and we could get this all taken care of.

"A sex club."

Well, that silenced them. All three stared at me.

"Not a strip club or something like that. Specifically, a BDSM club," I said. "I saw one in New York and thought that something similar would work well here."

"What club in New York?" Cai asked.

"Club Privé."

Slade grinned. "You're shitting me. You went to Club Privé?" He glanced at the other two. "I think we've finally found something we have in common."

TWENTY-EIGHT
SYLL

I reported the assault. If whoever had done it came back, I wanted to make sure the cops would take me seriously. They were annoyed that I hadn't come in right after the attack happened but became much more sympathetic after I explained that I couldn't afford to lose the time it would take for them to do all their questioning at the bar. As I was leaving, I saw a picture on one of the detective's desks, and the reaction made a lot more sense. He had a daughter who looked about my age, and she was standing in front of a diner, holding papers that said she owned the place. He must've been imagining how he'd want someone to help her if she was in a situation like mine. I hoped that also meant he'd put a bit of a priority on finding the bastard who was doing this.

Outside was still gray and gloomy, but it'd stopped snowing, and the temperature was back in the decent range for the end of January, which meant all my regulars had been back since Thursday night. I also had about a dozen new customers, and while I wasn't going to count on them coming back on a regular basis, I was grateful for their business.

My ribs still ached if I turned the wrong way, but I could see out of my left eye again, and the bruises were almost gone. A hot shower at the end of the night took care of most of the usual aches and sore muscles. All in all, I was in a good mood when I finally turned in around three in the morning.

I settled under the covers and breathed out a slow sigh. I knew I couldn't count on every day being as busy as today, and one profitable night wouldn't turn things around for me financially, but I allowed myself to hold on to that sliver of hope.

I could do this. I'd figure out new marketing strategies to reach a wider market. I'd research promotions and look in to what sorts of specials worked best in a place like this. Maybe I'd even talk to the bank and see if I qualified for a small business loan. As much as Jax's questioning had pissed me off, it'd made me think about expansion possibilities. If I had a better kitchen, I could offer a selection of food that could drum up some business.

I was exhausted, but even as I laid in bed, staring at the ceiling, my mind raced. Ideas and thoughts chased each other, jumping from one topic to another so fast that I could barely process one before another took its place. I would've preferred to sleep, but at least these thoughts weren't the negative, worrying ones that had plagued me daily since Dad died.

I was thinking through the possibilities of advertising on social media when I heard a noise from the bar. I stilled, unsure if I'd really heard it, or if I was imagining things because of everything that'd happened.

Then I heard it twice in a row.

It wasn't a loud sound, and it wouldn't have woken me up if I'd been asleep. I'd almost missed it awake. I couldn't quite place what it was. A soft, irregular thump that was too quiet for tipping chairs or breaking things, and not uniform enough for footsteps.

And it sure as hell wasn't the building settling or anything like that. Someone was in my bar.

I threw back the covers and reached for my phone. As I dialed, I crept out of my bedroom and into the main area.

"911, what's your emergency?"

"There's an intruder in my house." I wasn't whispering, but I kept my voice low. I had no way of knowing where the intruder was out there. The office between us might've acted as a buffer, but I wasn't going to count on it.

"Are you alone in the house?"

I nodded, then remembered the operator couldn't see me. "I am. I live in an area behind my bar. He's out in the bar."

"Stay where you are, miss," the operator said. She rattled off the address and then asked for confirmation.

"That's it." I took a step toward the door.

"The police are on their way."

"There's a Detective Lambert who's working on my case. Someone should call him."

I held the phone between my ear and shoulder as I pulled on a pair of shoes.

"What case?"

"Vandalism and assault. I was in yesterday to give a statement about a guy coming into my bar the other day and beating me up." I looked around, trying to decide what would make the best weapon.

"Do you have a way out that won't put you in the intruder's path?"

I glanced toward the door right next to my bedroom. "I have an emergency door, but it'll set off an alarm if I go out it, and it leads to an alley that's closed off by fences that're too tall for me to get over."

"Just stay where you are for right now then," the operator said. "If he comes back there though, you need to get out."

"Sure," I said absently as my gaze fell on a box of Dad's stuff I'd left in the corner of the room, unsure what to do with it. If I remembered correctly, one of the things in there was his fishing gear, including a boning knife. That'd do.

"I need to go."

"Stay on the line with me," she said.

"He might hear me."

I knew it was a cop-out reason, but I also knew she'd try to talk me out of what I wanted to do. I was tired of hiding, of being scared. My dad hadn't raised me to be a victim, and that was how I'd felt for the last couple days. I was through with it. I didn't care that it was stupid and rash, or that it might get me killed. I'd reached my limit.

As I dug in the box for the knife, my phone rang, startling me bad enough that I almost dropped it. I hit the accept button without even really registering who was calling. I just needed the phone to stop ringing before the guy in the bar heard it and came back to investigate.

I was just getting ready to end the call without speaking when I saw who it was. If I was going to do stupid things tonight, I might as well add one more to the list.

"Hello?"

"Syll, what's wrong? You didn't say anything. I thought I lost you."

I told myself not to take those words at anything but face value. "No, I'm here."

"Look, I need to talk to you. I didn't handle what happened well, and I want to explain–"

"Now's not a good time," I cut in. My fingers closed on the familiar handle and I held up the knife. "Yahtzee."

"Syll? Why are you whispering? I can barely hear you."

"Sorry, Jax. Someone's in the bar, and I can't let him hear me."

He cursed. "What are you still doing in there? Get out!"

"I can't," I said as I straightened. "If I go out the back, an alarm will go off and I'll get stuck in the alley. Sitting duck."

"Why aren't you on the phone with the cops?"

"I already called 911," I explained. "They're on their way."

"Where are you?"

"In the living room."

"Get back into your bedroom," he ordered. "Get under the bed and don't move until someone gets there. I'm on my way."

"Stay away," I said firmly. I desperately wanted him here, but I wasn't going to be selfish. "You could get hurt."

"*I* could get hurt?! Are you crazy?!"

The intensity in his voice made me smile. He really did care about me. What he'd said before had to have been just poor communication. Unfortunately, this wasn't the time or place for a discussion.

"It's okay," I said. "The cops are on their way."

"But you aren't going to wait for them, are you?"

The resignation in his voice almost gave me pause, but I shook it off. "Don't worry. I'll be fine."

"Don't do anything stupid, Syll. Please. Just go hide in your bedroom, in the bathroom, anywhere. Let the police do their job. I'm on my way."

I lifted my chin, even if he couldn't see it. "This is my home, Jax. And I'll be damned if I'm going to let some gutless bastard drive me out of it. He won't catch me off-guard this time."

"Syll." My name was a warning.

"I have to go now."

I ended the call before he could say anything else. I couldn't stay on the phone with him, no matter how good his concern made me feel. He'd try to talk me into hiding, and I'd probably let him. I didn't doubt he wanted what was best for me, but I had to do this. For me.

I had to prove to myself that I could defend what was mine.

No matter how stupid it was.

TWENTY-NINE

JAX

WHAT THE HELL WAS SHE THINKING?!

I nearly tripped as I pulled on the first pair of pants I could lay my hands on. I'd been in bed, not able to sleep, thinking about everything that'd happened over the last two days. Some of it had been about my brothers and the strange realization we'd all come to that afternoon about our involvement in BDSM, but even finding common ground with my brothers hadn't been enough to stop me from thinking about what happened with Syll.

It'd been a complete misunderstanding on her part, and I'd been stung that she'd thought so little of me. I'd never fucked someone to close a business deal, and I never would've done that to someone I...cared about.

I had to admit at least that much to myself. Otherwise, I wouldn't have been scrambling around to get dressed so I could go save her.

I called her on a whim, knowing she'd still be up. The plan had been to explain to her that I'd simply been admiring the space and thinking of ways she could build business because I knew it was something she worried about. I wasn't sure when it happened, but I'd stopped wanting to buy the bar. Not because I didn't think it was quality property anymore. It was still perfect for a club, and I still wanted to build one.

But that was all it was. I wanted to build a business that interested me. That's what the club was to me.

To Syll, her bar was her life.

And that was what had panic flooding me. The bar was her life, and she was going to defend it with her life.

She was going to get herself killed, and that wasn't acceptable. I didn't want to even think about a world without her in it.

I knew that meant I didn't simply *care* about her, but that wasn't something I had the luxury of analyzing at this moment. I had to get to her before it was too late. I'd figure the rest of it out after she was safe.

I started toward the parking garage but kept my eye out for a taxi. Whichever car I saw first, I'd take. I didn't even feel the bite of the air as I broke into a jog. A cab pulled up before I'd gone more than a few feet and I got into the back, giving the address before I even closed the door.

"I'll give you double the fare if you get me there in ten minutes or less."

I sat back and closed my eyes, knowing that the cabbie would be less likely to start up a conversation if he thought I was resting. I couldn't handle talking to him, not when I was trying so hard not to think of all the things that could be happening to Syll without me there.

I never should have let her kick me out that night. If my fucking pride caused her to get hurt because she was alone, I'd never forgive myself. I should have been there with her. Better yet, she shouldn't have been there at all. She should have been with me, at my house where I could protect her.

I promised myself that, as soon as I had the opportunity, I was going to make things right. I'd be honest with her about the things I wanted, and I'd tell her that we could come to some arrangement...

"Fuck," I muttered.

I didn't want an arrangement. I wanted *her*. She was tough and independent and smart-mouthed, all the things a Dom shouldn't want in a sub. Normally, I wouldn't either, but what I felt for her was different than what I'd felt for anyone else.

Different. Stronger.

I'd been miserable this week. Snapping at my brothers had just been the last straw. When I was with her, things weren't easy, but I felt like I could be me around her, more than I could be around anyone. Hell, half the time, I didn't really know who I was, and I definitely didn't like him. But when I was with her...

"You okay, Mister?" the driver asked. "You don't look so good."

I made a dismissive gesture that probably came off as rude, but I was too focused on the revelation that was slowly opening up in front of me.

I was falling for her.

No. I *had* fallen for her.

I was in love with Syll.

"What the hell is that?"

I didn't look up, not caring about whatever it was that had caught the cabbie's attention. A moment later, however, I did look up because we'd come to a stop. I handed over three twenties even as I opened the door. I stepped out into the cold night and noticed two things, one right after the other. The first was that there weren't any cops here yet. The second was that I'd seen what caught the driver's attention.

Smoke.

Thick smoke billowing out of the open door. Of the bar. Where Syll was.

I started forward, only to be knocked aside when someone came running out of the door. I caught a glimpse of Billy's panicked expression before I turned and ran inside. If he'd done something to Syll, I'd deal with him later.

The heat hit me hard, and I sucked in a breath. The smoke that was stinging my eyes filled my lungs, and I started to cough. I hunched over, trying to get to some of the cleaner air. It wasn't much better, but I could see where the flames were now. The entire right side was in flames, and the air was so thick with the smell of gasoline, I could taste it.

"Syll?!" I yelled her name as best I could. "Syll?!"

I ran into a chair and cursed. How was I supposed to see anything in here? I moved around it and spotted a dark shape on the floor. Syll was on her stomach, blood trickling from a cut on her temple. Her eyes were closed, and I couldn't tell if she was even breathing. I didn't want to think about that though. I needed to get her out of here, and then I could deal with whatever came next.

"I've got you." I scooped her up and started back to the door.

I was almost outside when the blast of an explosion hit me, and I stumbled forward, sharp pain blazing across my back and shoulders. I ignored it, taking the last few steps I needed to get us outside. I didn't stop there though. Behind me was a building full of alcohol that wouldn't fare well soon. I couldn't let Syll be anywhere near that.

I'd gone another half-dozen steps when I realized that I was hearing something other than the roar of flames in my ears. Sirens. A few moments later, two cop cars came screeching around the corner.

I ignored them and knelt on the sidewalk, still cradling Syll in my arms.

"Syll, you have to wake up, okay? There's so much I need to tell you." I brushed hair back from her face. "Please, Syll. Don't do this to me."

I only hoped I wasn't too late.

THIRTY
SYLL

It hurt to breathe. Like the sort of excruciating pain that made my bruised ribs feel like a pulled muscle. I coughed, the movement wrenching injuries that weren't quite healed. I made a pained sound, and that was when I realized that I wasn't on the floor of the bar. I was on someone's lap.

"Shh, easy. Slow breaths."

Jax?

Why was Jax holding me?

Wait, I'd called him. No, he called me. He said he was coming over.

"Open your eyes, sweetheart."

That did it. I blinked, tears filling my stinging eyes, then spilling down my cheeks. I frowned. Why was I crying? But I wasn't crying. Was I?

"There you are."

The relief in Jax's voice had me shifting my gaze to his familiar face. Familiar, and filthy.

"What happened?" Wow. Was that my voice? Why did I sound like a fifty-year-old chain smoker?

"What do you remember?" He shook his head even as he

asked the question. "Wait. Don't try to talk. You inhaled a lot of smoke."

Smoke? Why was there smoke?

I felt like I had smoke in my brain.

What happened? I remembered that I'd heard a noise and that I called the police. I talked to Jax, right before going out into the bar, armed with my dad's old boning knife.

The smell of gasoline had made my eyes water, but I'd still seen someone standing near the cash register. I'd taken just a step or two toward whoever it was when a burst of pain had exploded in my head, and everything had gone dark.

"Is my bar burning?"

I tried to sit up, and Jax wrapped his arm around my shoulders to help. When I was in an upright position, I found myself wishing that I'd kept my eyes shut.

My bar, my *home*, was burning. Two cops were shouting at a fire truck that was just now pulling up, but I knew they wouldn't be able to save it. The tears that streamed down my cheeks now had less to do with the smoke and more to do with the fact that I was watching everything I owned burn.

Everything my dad had ever owned or touched. Every memory I had of him. Every memento.

"I'm so sorry," Jax said as he held me. "I wish I could've done something to stop it."

A paramedic stepped into my field of vision. "Let's take a look at you two."

"I'm fine," Jax said. "Make sure she's okay."

The young man knelt in front of me and began going through all sorts of questions and tests. A light shone in my eyes. A stethoscope listening to my raspy breaths. But I wasn't really paying attention to anything he was doing. I just kept watching the fire.

Firefighters had hoses out now, but it didn't matter.

My home was gone.

"Miss, we need to get you to a hospital."

I shook my head, then coughed against Jax's shoulder.

"You should go, sweetheart," Jax said softly.

I barked out a laugh that sounded more like another cough. "When did you start calling me 'sweetheart?'"

"It's a long story," he said as he smoothed back my hair. "And I plan on telling you everything, as soon as you get checked out."

I glared at him. What the hell was he doing? I kicked him out after he'd tried to use sex to buy my bar out from underneath me. Why had he called me in the first place?

And why was he holding me on his lap like I meant something to him?

"No hospital," I said.

The paramedic sighed and held up a mask. "At least put this on while I take care of your boyfriend."

"He's not my boyfriend," I said, but the words were distorted by the mask, so I wasn't sure anyone understood me.

Or if it was even important.

The paramedic walked around behind Jax. "You're going to need to go to the hospital too."

"What happened to him?" I asked.

"Nothing," Jax said. "Don't worry about it."

"Is that glass from a whiskey bottle?" The paramedic's voice was incredulous.

I pulled the mask off. "What?!"

"Breathe," he insisted, putting the mask back on my face. "It's nothing."

I glared at him.

"One of the bottles exploded," he said. "That's all."

"No," the paramedic said. "That's not all. You have shards of glass stuck in your back."

"Can't you just take them out?" he asked, his tone impatient.

"You need to see a doctor."

"I have a friend who's a doctor," Jax said. "Just yank out the pieces, and I'll have him come by to stitch me up."

"Are you taking them to the hospital?" A cop came over, and Jax's arm tightened around me.

"They don't want to go."

"Well, I've never known anyone who could make Jax Hunter do something he didn't want to do," the cop said. "He's got quite the reputation in some circles."

"I'll get the paperwork," the paramedic said, resignation evident in his voice.

"While we're waiting for that, how about we get you two off the ground, and I'll take your statements while we wait."

I stood up, and the world spun. I would've fallen over if Jax hadn't caught me. As soon as he was on his feet, he picked me up. I tried to tell him that I was perfectly capable of walking, but it was only a few feet to the cop car, and then he was putting me on my feet.

He opened the back door and then, to my surprise, sat down, leaving his feet on the ground. I remembered the glass in his back and hoped he wouldn't forget and lean back.

Before I could offer to pull out the pieces, he reached for me and pulled me onto his lap. I should have stayed standing, or asked for another place to sit, but in that moment, I needed comfort.

And I wanted Jax to give it to me.

"All right, who wants to go first?"

"I will." My voice sounded so strange in my ears as I told him everything that had happened up until the point where I'd been knocked out. "If you talk to Detective Lambert, he'll get you up to speed on the rest of my case."

"Here," Jax said quietly. He helped me put the oxygen mask back on before he turned to the cop. "Like she said, I called her, and she told me that she heard someone in the bar. I told her to hide and that I was on my way. I caught a cab, and by the time I got here, there was smoke already coming out of the building. The front door was open."

He hesitated, and I felt him tense under me, telling me that there was something he didn't want to say out loud.

"Mr. Hunter?"

He glanced down at me, blowing out a deep breath. "I'm sorry, Syll."

What was he apologizing for this time?

"When I was heading inside to get Syll, someone came running out. He ran into me."

Even as the cop asked Jax if he recognized the guy, I knew what Jax was going to say.

"It was Billy Outhwaite," Jax said. He looked at me, another apology in his eyes.

"Who's Billy Outhwaite?"

"My ex-boyfriend," I volunteered the answer. "We broke up earlier this week."

"And you saw him too?"

"Hey, now," Jax leaned forward.

I held up my hand. "It's okay. It's a legitimate question." I turned back to the officer. "No, I didn't see him. I saw a figure, and then someone knocked me out from behind."

"So, he had a partner?"

I shrugged. "I don't know."

"He's been seeing one of the waitresses at the bar," Jax said. "Ariene something."

I gave him a sharp look, and he had the decency to look sheepish.

"Do you think she could have been with him?"

"I doubt it," I said. "She didn't strike me as the arsonist type."

"That's enough," Jax said as he put the mask over my mouth again. "You don't know how long you were breathing that shit."

"Mr. Hunter."

Jax looked up at the officer. "I'm not done with my statement. I'm sure you want to hear about how I went into a burning building and found her laying on the floor, knocked out and bleeding from that cut on her head. I picked her up and carried her out. And it took another five minutes for you guys to show up. What's up with that? Wrong part of town to get a quick response?"

My eyes widened.

"Mr. Hunter." The cop looked just as surprised as I was. "We ran into an accident. We couldn't get around it."

"I guess I'll just need to suggest to the commissioner that if he wants my continued support, he'll need to make certain more cars are assigned to this part of the city. If you guys had been doing your job in the first place, none of this would've happened."

"Jax." I put my hand on his cheek.

What was he doing?

"I-I think that's enough for now," the officer said as he took a step back. "If you think of anything else, please come down to the station. We'll give you a call, Miss Reeve, if we find anything."

He walked away, leaving us sitting in the back of his squad car alone.

I pulled off the mask. "What was that all about?"

"What?" Jax tried to put the mask back on, but I pushed it away. "You need to–"

"I'll make you a deal," I said. "If you tell me why you called me, I'll be good and keep the oxygen mask on until we sign whatever the paramedic has for us."

"Fine." He put the mask back into place. "I called you because I wanted to talk to you about what happened. I missed you this week. I've been miserable, and I thought you and I could talk about what this is between us."

What the hell?

"We can do that later, after we're safe at my place, clean and warm, and bandaged up." He took a slow breath, then looked directly into my eyes. "But I do want to tell you what I realized on the way over here."

My heart was suddenly pounding louder than the chaos around us.

"I'm in love with you, Syll, and I'm going to do whatever it takes to prove it to you."

Well, shit. I had *not* seen that coming.

THIRTY-ONE
JAX

I told Syll I loved her. I was still trying to wrap my head around that.

She hadn't said it back, but the paramedic had come over with the paperwork we needed to sign almost right after I'd said it, and by the time we were done with that, she looked so exhausted that I hadn't brought it up again. I could wait.

The police officer who'd taken our statements offered to drive us back to my place. If things hadn't been so insane, I would've been amused at riding in the back of the cop car, but as it was, all I'd been able to focus on was Syll. When we reached my house, she didn't protest when I told her she was staying with me, at least for now, but she did insist on walking rather than me carrying her.

While she was in the shower cleaning up, I called Harry Kingston, an ER doctor I'd met several years ago at a hospital fundraiser. Like me, he was a workaholic with little time for socializing, which meant we could consider each other a friend even though we rarely spent time together. And he was the sort of friend I could rely on in a situation like this.

By the time he left, both Syll and I had stitches – hers in her head, mine in my back – and she'd been given instructions to use the small tank of oxygen he'd brought with him. He promised to come back tomorrow to check on us, and then he left.

When Syll nearly fell face-first into her toast fifteen minutes later, I helped her up and into the living room. My house had plenty of beds available, but I wasn't sure I had the strength to get myself up the stairs, let alone help Syll. Now that the adrenaline had faded from my system, I was exhausted.

"Stay." She reached up and grabbed my hand. "Please."

"I'm just going over there." I gestured to a nearby chair with my free hand.

She shook her head. "Will you lay down with me?"

Maybe it was a bad idea since we hadn't talked about what I said to her, but I couldn't deny her, not when she needed me. It took some creative positioning for us to both fit without aggravating our injuries, but once we settled into place, I couldn't imagine anywhere else I'd want to be.

I'd put on a movie, but neither of us stayed awake much past the first few minutes, and when I woke up, I saw that nearly four hours had passed. My neck was stiff from how I'd been laying, and my arm was numb from Syll laying on it, but seeing how relaxed she looked, it was worth the discomfort.

Still, I needed to extract my arm, and despite the care I took, the movement woke her. She looked up at me, color flooding her cheeks.

I gave her a soft smile. "I'd say good morning, but I think it's actually afternoon now."

"Thank you," she said. Her voice still sounded a little rough, but it was better than it had been.

"For what?"

She gave me a look. "For saving my life. For bringing me back here so I didn't have to be alone."

She started to sit up, and I helped her until we were side-by-side in the middle of the couch. I wrapped my arm around her waist and pulled her as close as I could without her sitting on my lap again.

"May I ask a favor then?" I chose my words carefully. Not thinking before I spoke was part of what'd gotten me in hot water in the first place.

"All right," she said warily.

"Hear me out?" She nodded, and I continued, "I'm a businessman, and sometimes that's my default setting. It's how I see things. When I asked you about expanding your business, I swear to you, it was just an observation. Nothing manipulative or under-handed. Yes, I'd originally made an offer because I thought it was a perfect space for a club, and that's where my focus had been. But it's not there anymore. It hasn't been for a while."

I watched her face as she considered my words.

"I believe you."

I hadn't realized how tense I was until her words made me relax. I kissed the top of her head. "Thank you, sweetheart."

"Okay, what's with the *sweetheart*?" she asked, looking up at me. "You called me that before."

I hadn't realized I could feel embarrassed, but then again, I'd never been in love before. And I definitely hadn't confessed feelings to someone who hadn't said them back. If anything, I'd been on the other end of this situation. I didn't know how to handle the power shift here.

"I remember Billy calling you *babe*, and I wanted something different."

"But *sweetheart*? Really?"

"You don't like it?" The teasing tone helped ease the sting of her not liking the endearment I'd used.

She shook her head. "It just doesn't feel like...you."

"Then what should I call you?" To my surprise, I found myself teasing her right back. "Sugar? Honey? Darlin'?"

I drawled the last word and earned a laugh.

"None of those, please."

I reached down and cupped her chin, running my thumb along her bottom lip. "What then, my sweet, sweet Syll?"

She swallowed hard, though I didn't know if it was at the words or at the tone. "That-that's okay with me."

One side of my mouth curved up in a smile. "All right then, my sweet Syll, do you think we can talk about something on the serious side? If you aren't up for it, that's okay." I tucked some of her hair behind her ear and let my hand linger.

"Did you mean what you said before," she licked her lips, "about..."

"Me being in love with you," I finished for her. I brushed the back of my hand against the side of her face. "I'm not expecting anything. I just needed you to know."

She had a thoughtful look on her face, and I waited to see what she would say next. "What does that mean?"

"I'm not sure I understand."

"What does it mean to you to say that you're in love with me?" She sat up a little straighter but didn't pull away completely. "You said you don't have any expectations, but it has to mean something."

I was quiet for a few minutes, holding up a hand when she opened her mouth to say something. "I'm thinking. I've never said it before, so I've never had to explain it."

"I'm the only person you've said it to?" Her eyes were wide, her skin prettily flushed.

"You are," I admitted. "It's more than great sex or physical attraction. I've had those before. But I've never wanted to just spend time with someone. You challenge me, and you make me laugh, neither of which are easy things. I like being with you."

Her eyes sparkled. "Does that mean you don't want to have sex with me?"

"Hell no. I mean, yes. Shit." No one else ever managed to

fluster me. "Yes, I'm insanely attracted to you and would love to spend hours in bed showing you just how good I can make you feel, but I like this too. Watching a movie with you. Holding you. Talking to you."

"Where does this mean we go from here?"

I tried not to be disappointed that she still hadn't said how she felt about me. It'd hit me out of the blue. I couldn't expect her to have already gotten there. I'd just have to show her how good we could be together. I always rose to a challenge, and this would be no different.

"I'd like for it to mean we're dating." I tucked some hair behind her ear. "I won't ask you to be exclusive or offer any sort of commitment. You just got out of a relationship with Billy, and I don't want to be the rebound. Just know that I'm not planning on seeing anyone else."

She studied me for a moment. "What about sex?"

"What about it?"

"If I decide I want us to take things slow and don't want to have sex for a while, will that change things?"

"The only thing it'll change is how many cold showers I'll have to take."

She smiled at that.

"Seriously though, Syll. You set the pace, and you tell me what you want." She couldn't imagine how hard giving over control was, but she was worth it.

"And if I *do* want sex?"

A bolt of desire went right through me. "Then I'll be more than happy to comply." I paused, and then added, "That'd require a different sort of discussion though."

"What sort of discussion is that?"

I should have known she wouldn't want me to ease her into things. That wasn't who she was. "Before we get to that, I need to ask you something, and I need you to be completely honest with me."

She nodded. "I will."

"Are you still in love with Billy? I told you we'd go at your pace, and I meant it. I just want to know where I stand."

She leaned over and brushed her lips across mine. "My relationship with Billy has been on life support since long before I met you. Catching him with Ariene was just the kick in the ass I needed to pull the plug on it."

"All right," I said, trying not to show her how much I loved hearing that. "Then let's have the sex talk."

"I think I've already learned about the birds and the bees," she teased.

I gave her a long look, not speaking until she was practically squirming. "Not the way I do it."

SHE'D TAKEN the admission of my sexual preferences surprisingly well. In fact, her actual reaction had been: "Makes sense. No wonder you got off spanking me and bossing me around."

I'd gone over the basics with her, wondering the whole time if she'd decide it was too much, but with each new revelation, each answer to her questions, I saw nothing but interest...and desire.

Which was why I suggested that we distract ourselves by spending some time in my playroom.

She stood a few feet inside the room while I stayed back, drinking in the sight of her seeing it all for the first time. I tried to view it through her eyes. See the various shades of greens and blues that came together to form an ocean-like ambiance. I knew a lot of similar rooms were made up in blacks and reds, but I'd always loved the ocean.

A pair of chains hung from the ceiling in one corner, various opportunities for restraints attached to the walls closest to them. An X-shaped cross was fastened to the opposite wall, set-up in such a way that I could rotate it, even if someone was on it. A padded bench sat at the foot of the bed while my flogger and crop hung next to it, but I used them sparingly. Other types of restraints and toys were in the drawers under the bed. The bed itself was massive, with posts made for all kinds of bondage.

"I owe you two punishments." I broke the silence.

She half-turned. "Two punishments?"

"You disobeyed when I told you to keep your hands behind your back, and then you came without permission."

She opened her mouth, like she was going to argue with me, but I shook my head, and her jaw snapped shut. Her eyes gleamed with anticipation.

"Undress."

The clothes she'd been wearing when I found her were ruined, and I didn't keep women's clothes on hand, so she'd changed into a pair of my boxers and a t-shirt. Now, she pulled the t-shirt over her head, and slipped off the boxers, putting both on the bench.

"Do you remember the safe word we came up with?" I asked.

"*Sugar.*" She gave me a cheeky smile.

"On the bed. In the center. Lay on your back."

I watched her crawl into place, the tight muscles in her ass and thighs flexing as she moved. She settled on her back, eyes on me as I walked to each of the corners and placed restraints on her wrists and ankles. With the last one, she was spread-eagle, every inch of her exposed.

"I thought you were going to punish me," she said.

I reached down and flicked her nipple, watched it harden. "I am, but not like before. I'm not going to spank you. I think your body's taken enough abuse in the past week."

"Difference is," her eyes dropped to my lips, "I liked what you did."

When she was all healed, I was going to see just how much she liked it.

"You're going to like this too," I promised.

I crossed over to the chest of drawers and selected a few toys. I set them on the bed and then got out a condom. I didn't want to have to stop right in the middle of things to rummage through a drawer. I stripped off my clothes, enjoying the expression on her face as she watched. I didn't consider myself a vain person, but I liked the way she looked at me.

"Since this is your first time experiencing this sort of punishment, I'll go easy on you. Five minutes per punishment."

"Five minutes? That doesn't sound so bad."

"Just wait," I said, fight to keep my face serious. "You might change your mind."

"Bring it."

I laughed, the sound startling me. It'd been too long since laughter had been a part of sex for me. Yet another reason to love her.

"Remember, you asked for it."

I picked up a pair of clamps. They were beginner ones, with some padding and soft cloth. I had other kinds, including some with metal teeth sharp enough to draw blood. It wasn't time for those yet.

I leaned over her, taking one of her nipples into my mouth. She moaned and wiggled as I sucked on it, using teeth and suction to get it ready. When I raised my head, I brought my eyes to hers, and then closed the first clamp on her nipple. She gasped, her back arching, and I moved on to the other one, repeating the process.

"Five minutes," I said. "And trust me, taking them off won't provide as much relief as you think."

I wrapped my hand around my erection, giving myself a slow stroke, twisting my wrist over the head so I could use the pre-cum to ease the friction. I didn't speak as one minute turned into two, and Syll started to squirm. The movements made her breasts jiggle delightfully, and even more blood rushed into my cock.

"Okay," she said, her skin flushed. "You were right. Five minutes. It has to be five minutes, right?"

I glanced at the clock. "Three. You've got two more to go."

"Two more minutes?" She glared at me. "That can't be right."

"Would you like something to take your mind off them?" I asked, ghosting my fingers up her leg and across her belly.

"Yes," she said, her head bobbing as she nodded. "Yes, very much."

I picked up one of the other toys I'd selected but didn't show it to her. "You have five additional minutes of punishment. Do you want me to overlap them, or wait until those come off?"

She made a desperate sound. "Now! Please, Jax! I need something to distract me."

I gave her a wicked smile. "Don't forget, you asked for it."

THIRTY-TWO
SYLL

My nipples were on fire.

I couldn't take two more minutes of this. I knew I'd probably regret telling Jax to distract me with my second punishment, but all I could really think about at this moment was how much my nipples hurt.

I heard a low buzzing sound a second before the vibrator lightly touched my labia. The sensation immediately spread, then increased as he slipped the cool plastic between my lips, using the liquid from my pussy to smooth the way as he moved it up to my clit.

"Shit! Shit! Shit!" My curses changed focus when I saw Jax smirking at me. "This is not funny, you son of a bitch! Fuck! It's too much! Too much!"

I pulled on the restraints, but they were on nice and tight. I twisted and writhed, tried to close my legs, move out of the way, but nothing worked. I was stuck, desperate and aching, unable to get any sort of relief from the overwhelming sensations Jax was inflicting on me.

Then things got worse.

The vibrator slipped inside me, hitting a whole host of new

places. I waited for him to fuck me with it, but he didn't. He left it there.

Vibrating.

"I know you're having a hard time concentrating." Jax's voice cut through the haze. "But you need to know that you can come as much as you want."

He thought I was going to *come*? I was going to *explode*.

"I'm taking the clamps off now. Your five minutes is up for them. Three more minutes with the vibrator."

"Damn you," I nearly sobbed the words, but the cry turned into a scream as he pulled off the clamps and blood rushed into the sensitive flesh, bringing with it the sharp stabbing pain of re-introducing circulation.

Then his mouth was on me, tongue soothing my nipples even as he reached for the vibrator again. The moment it touched my clit, I came. And came. And came. Over and over, each wave pulling me under and over until I was drowning in pleasure. Until all my senses had blurred together, and I couldn't distinguish between sight and sound and smell and taste, and this was going to kill me...

I didn't realize I'd passed out until I started waking up. My skin felt too tight, my muscles twitchy. But I could hear again, and what I heard was Jax.

"You're fucking gorgeous when you come, my sweet Syll."

He was really going to call me that. The thought made me smile.

"Welcome back, sunshine."

I could live with that nickname too.

I opened my eyes and found Jax looking down at me. He brushed hair back from my face, and that was when I realized that my hands and feet were free. I frowned at him.

"What's wrong?" Concern chased away happiness. "Was it too much?"

I shook my head. "Why'd you untie me? You didn't come yet."

I could feel his erection against the small of my back.

"You're not used to being restrained for long periods of time." He smiled again and kissed my forehead. "Believe me, as soon as you're feeling up to it, I plan on seeing if I can make you pass out again."

I sat up despite my quivering muscles and maneuvered myself until I was straddling his lap. "I'm feeling as...up as you are." I reached down and caressed the thick shaft jutting up between us. Such soft skin over such a hard piece of flesh.

"Have you forgotten who's in charge here?" His words were tough, but the heat in his eyes said this was part of who he was and what we were doing.

I shook my head and smiled. "Just tell me what to do."

"Hands behind your back."

I obeyed, and the position put my breasts on display. I refused to feel any sort of shame though. There was nothing wrong with what we were doing.

He buried a hand in my hair, yanking my head back until I was staring at the ceiling. "Don't even think about disobeying this time."

"Then you shouldn't make punishments that are so much fun."

He wrapped his free arm around my waist and lifted me. He bit my throat, making me curse, and then pulled me down on his cock, hard enough to make me cry his name.

"That's right, my sweet Syll," he practically growled in my ear. "Scream my name."

And I did.

Until my throat was hoarse, and words no longer made sense.

But all of that was okay because he was there with me. The

man I loved. I was pretty sure, at one point, I told him that, but if I hadn't, I knew I'd tell him again soon. And more than once.

I WAS GETTING SPOILED, waking up in Jax's bed. It was Monday morning, and I'd been here since he brought me home on Saturday.

Home.

I didn't have a home anymore.

Tears pricked at my eyelids, and I rolled over, unable to appreciate the luxury of the high-thread-count sheets as I thought about everything I'd lost.

I hadn't gone back yet. The fire marshal hadn't deemed it safe. I doubted there'd be anything left though. I'd seen it on the news Saturday evening, and it'd burned to the ground.

I let out a shaky breath. I wasn't going to lay in bed and cry. I'd cried Saturday night, and Jax had held me. He hadn't tried to tell me that it was okay, or anything like that. He'd been there, and that had been more than enough.

Yesterday had been a nice day, and it'd felt like we'd been a normal couple, spending the weekend together. But today was Monday. A work day. And I didn't have a work to go to. And this wasn't my home.

I knew he'd never kick me out, but he and I needed to have a serious talk about where things would go from here. I'd called Gilly to tell her what happened and that I was okay. She'd told me I could stay with her, but she had a one-bedroom apartment that would fit in Jax's living room. Still, I at least had somewhere I could go if the situation started making things weird between Jax and me.

My phone rang, startling me. I'd shoved it into my pocket after I'd talked to Jax, so it'd survived the fire. Better than those clothes had, in fact.

I reached over and picked it up off the end-table. "Hello?"

"Miss Reeve, this is Detective Lambert."

I sat up. "Yes?"

"We've gotten some new information on your case. It's a bit much to go over on the phone, and we may have questions for you about it. Do you think you can come by this morning?"

I did a quick count of how long it would take me to shower, dress, and get to the station. "I can be there in thirty to forty-five minutes. Will that work?"

"Perfect. I'll see you then."

When I ended the call, I looked up to see Jax in the doorway.

"I thought you were going to the office."

He shook his head. "I wanted to see what you were doing today and if you needed me. I hired good people for a reason."

We'd done some clothes shopping for me yesterday, which meant I at least had some clothes to wear to the station that weren't Jax's, but there were things I needed to do. I just hadn't expected Jax to be there. I wasn't used to *anyone* being there anymore. Not like this, anyway.

"Detective Lambert wants me to come down to the station for an update, and maybe answer some questions."

"I'll come with you in case they want to talk to me too." He paused, then sighed. "I'm sorry, I shouldn't have invited myself along like that." He crossed over to me and kissed the top of my head. "I'm going to be an overprotective ass sometimes. I'm working on it."

I smiled and tilted my head back, so he could reach my mouth. The kiss was brief but thorough.

"I'll be coming back here afterward," I said. "I have to make a bunch of calls to schedule appointments and get information. The insurance company, all of the utilities, that sort of thing."

He crouched down, so we were at the same level. "Would you like me to come with you?"

I hesitated, and he reached out to put his hand on my knee.

"Be honest with me. I want to be there for you, but if you don't want me there, I won't go."

I took his hand and laced my fingers between his. "I'd like for you to come."

He smiled and nodded. "Then it's settled."

Forty minutes later, we walked into the police station, hand in hand. We asked the woman at the desk where Detective Lambert was and we were sent back to an interview room for some privacy.

We went through all the usual small talk as we got settled in our seats, and then we waited for the detective to tell us why we were here.

"We picked up Billy Outhwaite early this morning," he began. "He started blubbering before we could tell him that he was a person of interest, but not under arrest. He told us that he's been passing along information to a 'big scary guy' who wanted to convince you to sell the bar. He said he'd been told to come to the bar where he found this 'scary guy' pouring gasoline on everything. He says he was trying to talk the man out of burning the bar down when you, Miss Reeve, came out of your office."

Jax's fingers tightened around mine, and for a moment, I wasn't sure if he was comforting me, or if I was comforting him.

"He says the other man knocked you out. When he realized that the intention was to leave you in the bar after the fire was set, he tried to convince the other man to let him take you out, but his life was threatened. The man set the fire and headed toward the back of the bar, where Billy says there was an emergency back door. Afraid for his life, Billy ran, which is when you saw him, Mr. Hunter."

That was a lot of information to take in.

Billy had left me to burn.

"Obviously, he's lying."

I looked up. "What?"

Detective Lambert gave me a strange look, as if I should already know this. "He's clearly lying to cover his butt, and because he feels guilty. Now, he's a coward, but if he set the fire, he'd be guilty not only of arson but of attempted murder. The alley that the emergency door led to was closed in. Anyone who went out that way would've been trapped."

I shook my head. "Not necessarily. The guy who assaulted me was big enough, he could've gotten over the fence, no problem. As for Billy, him running and leaving me to die, sadly isn't that far-fetched. I've known him a long time, and as much as it hurts, I can believe that of him. I can't believe he'd knock me out and set a fire where he'd intentionally kill me. Honestly, I don't think he's brave enough."

"We're not blowing it off completely," the detective admitted. "We're on the look-out for someone who matches the description Billy gave us, but for right now, I want you to know you can breathe easier because Billy's in jail, and he won't be getting out anytime soon. You're safe."

THIRTY-THREE
JAX

If Billy was released from jail any time soon, he would be wise not to come anywhere near Syll or me, because after hearing confirmation of what he'd done, I'd probably put him in the hospital. I knew the cops weren't sure if he was lying about the involvement of another guy, but I tended to believe him. Not because I thought he was truthful, but because the man who'd hurt Syll before hadn't been Billy. Then, there was the fact that I didn't think Billy had the guts to do something like set the bar on fire, let alone with Syll in it. In my opinion, running away was just as bad, but it fit what I knew of his personality better than him being an active participant in murder.

I didn't share any of this with Syll though. She hadn't said much after we left the station, and I could tell she was still trying to work through what we learned. No words, no matter how carefully chosen, would be able to ease the pain of learning about Billy's betrayal. Cheating, she could chalk up to immaturity, to sex, to not wanting to commit. Being involved in a plan to take her bar by any means necessary was something else entirely, especially since Billy had always known how important it was to her.

I squeezed her tighter and kissed the top of her head. Whatever she needed to do to process, I would help, even if it meant letting her do it alone. I wasn't going to fuck this up again.

It was well past noon by the time we made it back to my house. I thanked our driver, and then followed Syll up the stairs to my door. I had to unlock it, so I didn't notice that we weren't alone until someone spoke.

"Don't try anything stupid."

The man had at least three or four inches on me, and a good fifty pounds or more. His face was the kind that screamed *thug* even without the scar running down the left side of his face. None of that was the reason I froze though. It was because he had a gun pointed right at Syll, and far too close for me to hope he'd miss if he pulled the trigger.

"I don't keep much cash on hand, but I'll give you what I have, as well as whatever else you want." Even as I said it, I knew he wasn't here to rob me.

"Let's get a little further inside," he said, gesturing with his gun. "I don't want either of you getting any ideas about trying to run out the door."

I gave Syll a gentle push, and she walked in front of me, allowing me to keep between her and the gun. My mind raced, trying to find an escape that didn't end with us getting shot in the back.

We sat on the couch next to each other, and Syll reached over to take my hand. Her fingers were cold, and I gave her what I hoped was a comforting squeeze.

"All right. I need you to give me honest answers, or I'm going to have to get creative with my asking."

He stood far enough away that he'd be able to react if I rushed him, but close enough that any shot was guaranteed to cause some damage.

"Where's Outhwaite?" He looked at Syll. "Is the coward hiding?"

"He's in jail," I said quickly, drawing his attention back to me. "The cops picked him up earlier today. He's told them about you. If you leave now, you can probably get a good head-start."

The thug shook his head, his disgust written on his face. "I knew getting him involved was a bad idea. First, he starts saying how he'll only give information, that he won't get hands-on. Then, after the last time I visited you, he gets all pissy with me, trying to tell me how to do my job." He rubbed the back of his hand across his forehead. "Fucking pussy started crying when I knocked you out, going on about how he hadn't signed up for this."

"Why?" Syll asked. "What's so important about my bar? Or, I'm guessing it's the land not the bar, because if you wanted the building, you wouldn't have torched the place."

"Don't you worry about that," the thug said. He reached into his pocket and pulled out some folded papers. "Cuz you're going to sign this."

"The property's worth is going to be going up soon because of some new developments in the area," I explained quietly. "That's how I found out about your bar. It was one of several businesses my grandfather wanted me to check out."

"Doesn't matter," the thug cut in. "She's going to sign over the property now."

"Do you really think anything you make her sign under duress is going to hold up in court?" I asked, trying to get his eyes back on me. "Or are you hoping your boss will be satisfied enough that you'll be able to cut and run before things get too complicated?"

"I told you to stay away from him." The other man ignored me. "My boss sent a man with a nice offer, and you got plenty of warning. You didn't listen. You don't have anyone but yourself to blame."

"Mr. Jones works for your boss too," Syll said, glaring up at the thug. "I'm not signing shit."

"You'll sign, or I'll shoot you both. I'll start with him, and I'll make it real painful." The gun swung over toward me. "Two kneecaps and gut shot. That's three chances for you to change your mind."

"Fuck you," Syll said with a smile.

He shrugged. "If that's how you want to play it. I'm sure your sugar daddy here is going to be real pissed at you when his knee explodes."

"Jax Hunter!" A woman's voice came from the front door. "If you're keeping my friend from answering her phone, I'm going to kick your..."

Whatever threat Gilly intended to make trailed off as she appeared in the doorway. Her wide eyes darted to me, to Syll, and then back to the gun.

I registered all of this as background information because as soon as the man turned away from Syll and me, I was on my feet. I grabbed the lamp from the table next to me and slammed it down on the thug's head. For a moment, I thought it hadn't done any good, but then he swayed, stumbled, and fell to the floor face-first. I kicked the gun to the other side of the room and put a knee in his back, just in case.

"What the fuck?" Gilly ran over to Syll.

"It's okay," Syll said. "It's okay now. Thank you for distracting him."

The blonde glared up at me. "Okay, I want to know what the fuck is going on here, and I want to know now. Syll gets beat up, and the bar burns down, and then I hear Billy's been arrested, then this? I'll say it again. What. The. Fuck."

"It's a long story," Syll said as she let Gilly help her up. "But first we need to call the cops."

Gilly looked down at the thug, drew back her foot, and kicked him in the head with the sort of kick I would've expected from a soccer player. If he hadn't been out already, that would've done it.

I was tempted to ask her to do it again.

"Let's wait outside," Syll said, taking her friend's arm.

"Good idea." I met Syll's eyes. "And after we call the cops, I'll call a hotel for a suite."

"A hotel?" Syll asked.

"Your place isn't exactly livable, and mine's about to be a crime scene," I said wryly.

She blew out a breath. "Right."

As I dialed 911, she bent down and kissed my cheek before snuggling against my side. I hated that she'd been hurt, but I couldn't deny that I was finding the idea of my future a hell of a lot brighter than it had been before I'd met her.

THIRTY-FOUR
JAX

It was good to be home, I thought as I left my bedroom and headed downstairs to pick up my mail.

Technically, the police had cleared my place after just two days, but Syll and I had stayed at the hotel for the remainder of the week while my new security team installed new cameras, new locks, and a whole host of other security measures. I'd been promised that it all came with a money-back guarantee that no one would be able to bypass the security system. Their background checks were thorough, and their other customers satisfied.

We'd come back a week ago, and it still surprised me at how well the two of us had settled into living together. I'd never thought I'd want to live with anyone, but with Syll, it felt natural. We teased and bickered, but I didn't feel like she was intruding on my space. In fact, I loved that she'd already found little ways to make her presence known.

Her shampoo and soap in the master bathroom. Her toothbrush next to mine. The new clothes I'd talked her into letting me buy – she insisted that she'd pay me back, but I wasn't going to let her – and her shoes by the front door. A copy of an Ursula K Le Guin book on the end table on her side of the bed.

Now I just had to convince her that I wanted her to stay... and hope that's what she wanted too. I had a plan for today, and it was making me jumpy, even after I'd worked out some of the tension in my personal gym, first with some weight lifting, and then by bending Syll over the weight bench and fucking her senseless.

She was currently in the master bathroom, showering after the unplanned sex marathon in the gym. I'd used the shower there because now that things were getting down to the wire for me to put my plan into place, I was worried that I'd spoil the surprise if I'd climbed into the shower with her.

At least things were going well with the investigation. Billy had cut a deal and positively identified the thug as the man who'd hired him. In turn, the thug had flipped on Mr. Jones, who'd named a less-than-scrupulous rival of mine as his employer. More than likely, none of them would end up in court, which was more than fine by me as long as they served time. I didn't want Syll to have to deal with those guys any longer than necessary.

The mail came early on Saturdays, so it was already in a pile just under the mail slot when I walked into the foyer. I picked it up and began to shuffle through it absently. I received most of my bill statements via email, so what came via the post office was generally junk, but I never liked to just pitch it without looking through it first, just in case.

Credit card offer. Insurance offer. Catalog for fishing equipment for a Jack Hunt. Credit card offer. Loan offer. A seed catalog for a Miss Jay Hunter.

I loved mailing lists.

The last envelope was different from the others. It was still a business-sized envelope, but there was no return address. And the delivery address was handwritten. To me. In handwriting familiar enough to make me lose my breath.

I dropped the rest of the mail right back onto the floor and walked into the living room without taking my eyes off my name, almost frightened that if I did, it would disappear.

I opened it to find a neatly folded piece of paper inside. My chest was tight, my hands shaking, but I took the paper out and unfolded it. If I waited until I was ready to read it, I knew I never would.

Jax,

Upon the event of my death, I have asked Mr. Constantine to send this to you. I will spare you any sentimentality, as I know that we are both unaccustomed to such displays between us. This letter is not to explain the changes to my will, though I am sure they came as a surprise to you and your brothers. I know that you will come to understand them with time.

The purpose of this letter is to explain something that I have never spoken of to anyone outside of Mr. Constantine.

Bartholomew Constantine is a private investigator. I hired him twenty years ago to investigate the car crash that killed your parents and sister. I do not believe that it was an accident, and now that I am gone, I ask that you continue the search for the truth.

When I finished the letter, I went back and read it again. And again.

But the words just couldn't compute.

Because they were crazy.

They couldn't be real. None of this could be real. The accident wasn't an accident? Grandfather wasn't given to flights of fancy. But he'd hired a PI. And he'd been sure enough that he sent me a letter to make sure I kept up the investigation.

"Jax?"

I looked up to see Syll coming into the room. She wore one of my robes, the soft flannel dwarfing her. I patted the seat next to me, and she came over and sat down, a concerned expression on her face.

"What's wrong?" Concern filled her eyes. "You look like you saw a ghost."

"In a way I did." I held up the letter but couldn't bring myself to hand it to her. "It's a letter from my grandfather."

"Really?"

"Apparently, he hired a private investigator years ago because he didn't think the accident that killed my parents was an accident."

"What?" She put her hand on my arm.

"Yeah, I'm as surprised as you are. He never talked about it, never gave me a hint that he ever thought it was something other than a car accident."

"How much do you remember?" she asked gently.

"Not much." I shook my head. "I was a kid, so no one wanted to tell me much about what happened, and I didn't want to upset Grandfather, so I never asked. The more time that passed, the less I thought about it."

She ran her fingers through my hair, her touch soothing. I leaned into her, needing the comfort even if I didn't want to admit it.

"Cai, Slade, and I were at a friend's house when it happened. We didn't know until it was all over. Grandfather came from the hospital after...it was over, sat us all down, and told us that our parents and sister were dead and that Blake was going to be okay. He just said it was a car accident."

"That's awful."

I looked over at her now and saw tears in her eyes.

"I never knew he thought it was anything else. Why didn't he tell me?"

She squeezed my hand. "Maybe he didn't want to burden you with it."

I gave her a half-smile. "Trust me, protecting me wasn't something Grandfather really did."

"Yes, he did," she countered. "I'm sure he didn't want to tell you until he knew for certain what happened. He didn't want you to have the pain of not knowing."

She leaned forward and kissed my forehead. I wrapped my hand around the back of her neck and pulled her to me. I could feel my desperation in the kiss, but I didn't feel the need to hide anything I was feeling. She understood without me needing to say a word.

I'd contact this Constantine fellow and get the facts. If I thought he was on the level, I'd do what my grandfather asked and continue to look for the truth.

I'd just wait to tell my brothers. No point in bringing up painful memories if there wasn't anything there.

THIRTY-FIVE
SYLL

Tomorrow was Valentine's Day, but I wasn't expecting anything since Jax had already done so much for me. Besides, we hadn't even really solidified that we were in a relationship until last week.

I thought we might go out to eat, or order in something special. What I hadn't expected was him to say we were going out, especially after everything he'd just learned. He'd said a distraction was exactly what he needed, and of course, I hadn't been able to deny him. The weather wasn't bad, at least. Cold, but not bitterly so.

As the car pulled up to the curb, I caught my breath. "I hadn't realized they'd cleared it already."

"I may have mentioned a bit of incentive if they finished the job before today." Jax held out a hand to help me out of the car.

I stood in front of the lot and stared at the place where my home used to stand. I'd come by once after the fire, but the sight of the charred bones of the building had been too much. Now, it was smooth ground, everything gone.

"I also hired men to salvage anything they could. It's being packed away for whenever you feel up to going through it."

"Thank you." I gave him a tight smile, emotion clawing its way up my throat. "It's just hard to believe it's gone, you know."

He put his arm around my waist and pulled me to his side. "I do know."

If anyone knew what it was like to have something there one day and gone the next, it was Jax.

"We haven't really talked about what you want to do," he said. "You have the insurance money, but that doesn't mean you have to rebuild."

I leaned my head on his shoulder. If that wasn't an invitation to tell him the idea I'd had floating around in my brain, nothing was.

"I think I might like to rebuild, but not as a bar. And I might need a partner for what I have in mind."

I felt him stiffen as my words sank in. "Syll, are you sure that's what you want?"

I pulled away enough to look up at him. "I am. If you still want to build a club here."

"I do," he said. "And I would love for you to be my partner."

I threw my arms around his neck and kissed him soundly on the mouth. Instead of deepening the kiss, however, he raised his head.

"My sweet Syll, I brought you here to talk about the future, but not just the future of your business." He brushed back my hair. "I want to be your partner in everything."

I stared at him. What was he talking about?

"I know this is going to sound crazy, but I want you to live with me. More than that, I want to marry you."

"Are-are you serious?"

He smiled widely. "I am. And if you'll let me go, I'll get the ring out of my pocket."

Holy shit. He wasn't kidding.

I COULD FEEL the cool metal of my engagement ring on my finger, but I still couldn't believe it. I couldn't believe that I was engaged to a man I'd known for only a month. A billionaire who was going to be my partner in every way.

And that wasn't all I couldn't believe.

My current position was also more than a little unbelievable.

I was on my knees, bent forward so that my cheek was on the soft carpet. My arms were stretched out behind me, legs spread wide so every bit of me was exposed. But I couldn't change any of that thanks to the leather cuffs connecting my wrists to my ankles.

Not that I would've wanted to change anything. Not with Jax going to his knees behind me, his cock hard and bare. When he asked me what I wanted to do to celebrate our engagement, I told him that I wanted to feel him inside me with nothing between us.

He'd fingered me to two climaxes in the back of the car before we'd gotten home, and then we'd gone straight to the playroom, where he'd stripped me and tied me up.

That had been ten minutes ago, and I was still wet and ready for him.

He grasped my hips, the tip of his cock nudging my entrance. The anticipation had my entire body tight and quivering, so when he buried himself inside me with one hard thrust, I felt it in every cell of my body. I let out a cry that became a wail when he set a punishing pace, driving the air from my lungs and all reason from my brain.

My mind scrambled to keep up with all the sensations coursing through me, but the one word that dominated my thoughts was *love*. All-encompassing, all-consuming. A fire that burned through me faster, brighter, and hotter than anything I'd ever felt before.

Pressure coiled in my belly, tightening every time Jax

bottomed out. With my hands restrained, my climax was completely in his hands, but I trusted him not to leave me unsatisfied. Then he worked a thumb into my ass, and all I could do was whimper.

His hips jerked, rhythm faltering, and then he was coming, emptying inside me as his fingers dug into my hips. With a groan, he draped himself across my back. He moved one hand beneath me to where our bodies were still joined, fingers finding my clit, skillfully manipulating it until I came with a shout.

"My sweet, sweet Syll," he murmured as he pressed a kiss to my skin.

"I love you," I said when I could manage words. "And I can't wait for us to start our life together."

"I love you, too. And that life is going to begin with me spending the rest of today, and all of tomorrow, showing you just how much I love you."

As he reached down to unhook the cuffs, I took the opportunity to let my body come down from the high he'd given me. "I'm looking forward to it."

Every last minute of it.

The End

The Hunter Brothers continues in Cai's story, *His Control*, releasing March 28th. Turn the page for a preview.

HIS CONTROL – PREVIEW

PROLOGUE

Manfred

I wasn't sure which was worse, watching my beloved Olive standing by the portraits of our son, daughter-in-law, and granddaughter while sobs shook her frail shoulders, or seeing my grandsons standing next to her, each face heart-breakingly stoic. All except for Blake. He'd been furious with the world from the moment he'd woken up in the hospital, and nothing Olive or I had been able to do had changed that.

A part of me still felt like this was all some horrible nightmare, that I'd wake up and find my wife sleeping peacefully next to me. She'd tell me that none of it was true, that Chester and Abigail were safe at home with Aimee and the boys. I'd go back to sleep, making plans to see them all soon so I could put this terrible dream to rest.

Except, only the real world could hurt this much.

And it couldn't be a nightmare because that would've meant I'd been able to sleep. In the past few days, I'd barely managed twenty or thirty minutes a night. Every time I closed my eyes, I was back in the hospital, standing next to my son's bed, listening to the doctor tell me that he'd never wake up, that I had to decide if I wanted to keep his body alive, or let him go. Or I was in the morgue, identifying Abigail and Aimee, both barely recognizable.

As awful as that had been, the worst moments were when I had to tell the boys. Blake was only four. He didn't really understand what it meant that his parents and sister were gone. For him, I didn't think it had sunk in that they would never return. Slade was only a year older, but he was starting to put things together. When I tried to leave the house yesterday to come here and deal with the paperwork that inevitably came with death, he wrapped his arms around my leg and begged me not to leave. When Jax had come over to get him, Slade had started screaming that if I left, I'd never come back.

I watched Jax now as he leaned over to Slade and fixed his brother's tie. He'd been helping with his brothers, most of the time without even being asked. I hated seeing such a weight on his little shoulders, but I didn't know how to tell him it was okay to just be a kid. I'd never been someone who'd expressed emotions easily. Olive had always been best at that, and Chester had been like her.

I was just grateful that I wasn't doing this alone.

"Mr. Hunter." Officer March drew my attention away from the boys. "If I could have a moment of your time."

I shook his hand, then motioned for him to follow me away from the long line of people still waiting to offer their condolences. Chester and Abigail had been well liked, and everyone had loved Aimee.

"I'm sorry to approach you like this," he said, pitching his voice low enough that no one else could hear. "But I've been ordered to close the case and stay away from you."

It took a moment for his words to process. "What, exactly, do you mean?"

Officer March scratched the back of his head, his eyes

darting around as if he was still worried about someone overhearing us. "My partner wasn't too keen on me telling you that I thought what happened was no accident."

"I remember," I said, my heartbeat increasing its rhythm, "but I believed you would be investigating anyway."

He nodded. "I was. I *did*, actually. I visited the crash site again. Looked over the autopsy reports. Something was off, but I was still trying to figure it out when my captain called me into his office and told me that I needed to stop stepping on the detectives' toes." Another furtive look around. "The thing is, I spoke with the detectives yesterday, and they told me that they were getting ready to sign off on the accident report. My asking questions apparently made it look like they weren't doing their job." He looked away and then back again. "Or, at least that's what my boss said."

"You don't think that's the case?"

"I think someone doesn't want anyone looking too closely at the accident."

I shifted on my feet, my mind racing. I'd been going over this in my head every moment that hadn't been consumed with planning and business. A true accident – black ice, an animal crossing the road – would be awful, but the idea that someone had done this on purpose...it was unimaginable. What sort of person could put a plan into motion that wouldn't only leave a family without their father, but almost guaranteed collateral damage? I knew that Chester's investigative journalism had created enemies, but I doubted any of them had the impudence to take a life.

Still, despite all of those doubts, my gut said there was more to what happened than most people were seeing. I hadn't managed a multi-billion-dollar business from the time I was twenty relying only on visible logic. I'd always had good intuition, and now it was telling me that something smelled fishy.

But I was still going to be smart about it.

"What makes you think that you can't take the request from your captain at face value?" I knew Captain Hartman, and he was usually a straight-shooter.

"Because the order about staying out of the case wasn't all he said." Officer March leaned closer. "He told me to stay away from you specifically, that you didn't want me poking around in things."

My stomach sank. I hadn't spoken to Hartman about Officer March. In fact, the only conversation we'd had since the crash was when Hartman said, "It's a hell of a thing, losing members of your family like that."

Fucking understatement of the century.

"You're right," I said, pressing a hand to my roiling belly. "Something isn't right about it."

"If I keep looking into this, it could be my job," he said. His eyes were wide. "What do you want me to do?"

I scrubbed a hand across my chin.

"Grandfather." A tug on my sleeve made me look down as much as Cai's quiet voice. His little face was solemn, bright blue eyes clear. "May I be excused?"

I swallowed hard against the lump in my throat and nodded. Cai didn't run off. He walked, calmly and like he knew exactly where he was going and why. It wasn't a seven-year-old way of doing things, but Cai had never been a normal child. Out of all of my grandchildren, he was the one who reminded me the most of myself. Focused and serious, never showing how he felt about anything. Not even after losing three members of his family.

"How are they?" Officer March asked. "I mean, I know they aren't fine, not after what happened, but...dammit. You know what I mean."

I nodded. I did know. "They're as good as can be expected."

Cai disappeared around the corner, and I found myself wondering where he was going, and if I might join him. Cai had asked if he could go back to school this week, and I understood the sentiment. It had been difficult this week not to throw myself into work, escape that way.

"Mr. Hunter," Officer March spoke again. "What would you like me to do?"

I didn't look at him as I answered, "I don't want you to lose your job."

I heard his sigh of relief over the chatter around me.

"I'd hoped you'd understand." His hand touched my arm, and I turned to see him holding out a piece of paper. "I took the liberty of writing down the name and contact information of a private investigator I know. He's a good guy. Knows his shi-stuff, and he's discreet."

I glanced down at the paper before putting it in my pocket.

Bartholomew Constantine.

After all of this was done, I'd give him a call, see if he could find anything.

If there was anything worth finding.

ONE
CAI

Twenty-Four Years Later

I SHOVED MY CARRY-ON INTO THE OVERHEAD BIN AND wondered if I'd made a mistake in not asking my brother if the company plane could fly me back to Atlanta. I wouldn't have asked him to arrange a private plane again, not when it wasn't an emergency, but the company plane belonged to Hunter Enterprises, and since part of my trip had been spent dealing with issues related to the business, I could've justified it to myself.

Who was I kidding?

No, I couldn't have.

I felt guilty even thinking about the meeting with Germaine Klaveno, Grandfather's attorney, as business. It had pertained to the company, but only because the inheritance of Grandfather's shares – as well as the rest of the estate – were dependent on a few things.

Like my brothers and I reconciling our differences.

I folded myself into the window seat and mentally cursed myself for not being willing to wait one more day for an aisle seat. Coach seats weren't made with a six-feet, five-inch frame in mind, but I couldn't justify the expense of a first-class seat for a two-and-a-half-hour flight. Not when my money could be better spent elsewhere. The clinic where I volunteered was always short on funding. The cost differential between a coach ticket and a first-class ticket could mean the difference between the clinic getting an X-ray machine that actually worked, and continuing to make do with one that gave fuzzy exposures half the time.

"That doesn't look very comfortable."

The woman looking down at me had tight gray curls, a blue cardigan, and those glasses with a chain that hung around her neck. Even though she looked nothing like my Grandma Olive, she had the same sort of caring, sweet air about her, and my throat closed up with the sudden memory.

She sat down in the aisle seat but stayed perched on the edge. "You know, whenever I fly out to see my son, I always buy an extra seat for my Sherlock."

I gave her a tight smile. It didn't matter if Sherlock was a dog or a cat, I'd be polite and not complain, even when I started sneezing.

"Except I had to put him down a few months back, and when I bought my tickets, I plum forgot that I only needed one."

Where was she going with this? It took all of my patience to bite my tongue and wait for her to get to the point. Usually, I had extraordinary patience, but after spending this past week with my brothers, it was wearing thin.

"You see, what I'm wondering is if you wouldn't mind switching seats with me." She gave me that grandmotherly smile again. "I think if I was by a window, I wouldn't be thinking about my poor Sherlock. You'd be doing me a favor, sitting out here on the aisle, with an empty seat between us."

I nodded, unable to speak just yet. I couldn't remember the last time someone had done something kind for me without any thought of what they could receive in return. She might be saying that I was doing her a favor, but we both knew who was helping who.

When we were all settled in our new seats, I looked over at her. "Thank you."

She reached over and patted my arm. "Don't mention it, dearie. You looked like you've been having a rough time of it lately."

She had no idea.

I knew Grandfather had done the best he could, raising us boys. Grandma Olive had made things easier, but she passed only four years after my parents and sister, another blow to our already fragile family. Instead of everything we'd been through bringing us together, it had pushed us apart, each for our own reasons. But it didn't mean his death hurt any less.

"Pardon me."

I looked up as a flight attendant leaned over me to put something in the overhead compartment. She was pretty, probably a few years younger than me, and smiling down at me in a way I easily recognized. I didn't have the money that Jax and Blake possessed, or Slade's charm, but I wasn't hurting for it either, which usually made things worse when it came to women. Between my looks – a fluke of genetics – and my job – which I'd worked my ass off to get – I wasn't hurting for female attention.

The flight attendant closed the compartment and shifted her position to allow a line of passengers to go by. The fact that it pressed her right up against my arm and shoulder wasn't intentional at all, I was certain. I resisted the urge to roll my eyes. I appreciated confident people but brazen wasn't an attractive quality, in my opinion.

"Is there anything I can get you?" she asked, her dark eyes making the invitation out to be more than the usual peanuts and sodas.

"No, thank you," I said politely as I picked up my book.

"Whatcha reading?" The attendant rubbed against my arm with all the subtlety of a cat in heat.

"*Infectious Disease Precautions and Protocols in Urban Environments,*" I said lightly. "I'm on the chapter about quarantine in areas with rodent infestations."

Horror and disgust were almost immediately covered by a plastic smile, but I knew I wouldn't need to worry about her bothering me for anything other than her usual duties.

"Are you a doctor?"

I turned to my seatmate to find her watching me with an amused expression on her face.

"Yes," I said. "My specialty is infectious diseases."

"I'm going to go out on a limb here and assume that you work for the CDC." She reached into her bag and pulled out a piece of hard candy. "You could have just told her to leave you alone because you needed to concentrate on an important case."

I shrugged. "The truth seemed like a simpler and more logical deterrent than coming up with a story that might only pique her interest."

The older woman held out another piece of candy. I took it and popped the peppermint into my mouth.

"Were you in Boston for business or pleasure?" she asked.

"Neither," I answered honestly. "My grandfather died."

Her face softened, and she reached over to pat my hand. "I'm sorry to hear that, dearie."

I gave her a tight smile. "Thank you."

The voice of the head flight attendant came over the intercom just then, interrupting any further attempt at a conversation for the moment. I leaned my head back and closed my eyes. I'd flown enough to know the speech given at the beginning of every flight. If I could clear my mind for a few minutes, I could be asleep before take-off and wouldn't wake up until we started our descent.

Except I couldn't clear my mind, and it wasn't the fault of

the flirting flight attendant, or the kind, older woman. For once, it wasn't even my work that had my head buzzing.

No, it was those infernal requirements Grandfather had put on the distribution of his estate. My brothers and I had known that going our own ways was in everyone's best interests, and Grandfather hadn't said a word to the contrary. Why had he decided that, after his death, we should suddenly come together as a family?

We hadn't been a true family for nearly twenty-five years.

Continues in *His Control*, the second book in the Hunter Brothers series.

ALSO BY M. S. PARKER

Big O's
Rescued by the Woodsman
Sex Coach
The Billionaire's Muse
Bound
One Night Only
Damage Control
Take Me, Sir
Make Me Yours
The Billionaire's Sub
The Billionaire's Mistress
Con Man Box Set
HERO Box Set
A Legal Affair Box Set
The Client
Indecent Encounter
Dom X Box Set
Unlawful Attraction Box Set
Chasing Perfection Box Set
Blindfold Box Set
Club Prive Box Set
The Pleasure Series Box Set

Exotic Desires Box Set

Pure Lust Box Set

Casual Encounter Box Set

Sinful Desires Box Set

Twisted Affair Box Set

Serving HIM Box Set

ABOUT THE AUTHOR

M. S. Parker is a USA Today Bestselling author and the author of over fifty spicy romance series and novels.

Living part-time in Las Vegas, part-time on Maui, she enjoys sitting by the pool with her laptop writing her next spicy romance.

Growing up all she wanted to be was a dancer, actor and author. So far only the latter has come true but M. S. Parker hasn't retired her dancing shoes just yet. She is still waiting for the call to appear on Dancing With The Stars.

When M. S. isn't writing, she can usually be found reading– oops, scratch that! She is always writing.

For more information:
www.msparker.com
msparkerbooks@gmail.com

ACKNOWLEDGMENTS

First, I would like to thank all of my readers. Without you, my books would not exist. I truly appreciate each and every one of you.

A big THANK YOU goes out to all the Facebook fans, street team, beta readers, and advanced reviewers. You are a HUGE part of the success of all my series.

Also thank you to my editor Lynette, my proofreader Nancy, and my wonderful cover designer, Sinisa. You make my ideas and writing look so good.

Printed in Great Britain
by Amazon